Take Joy!

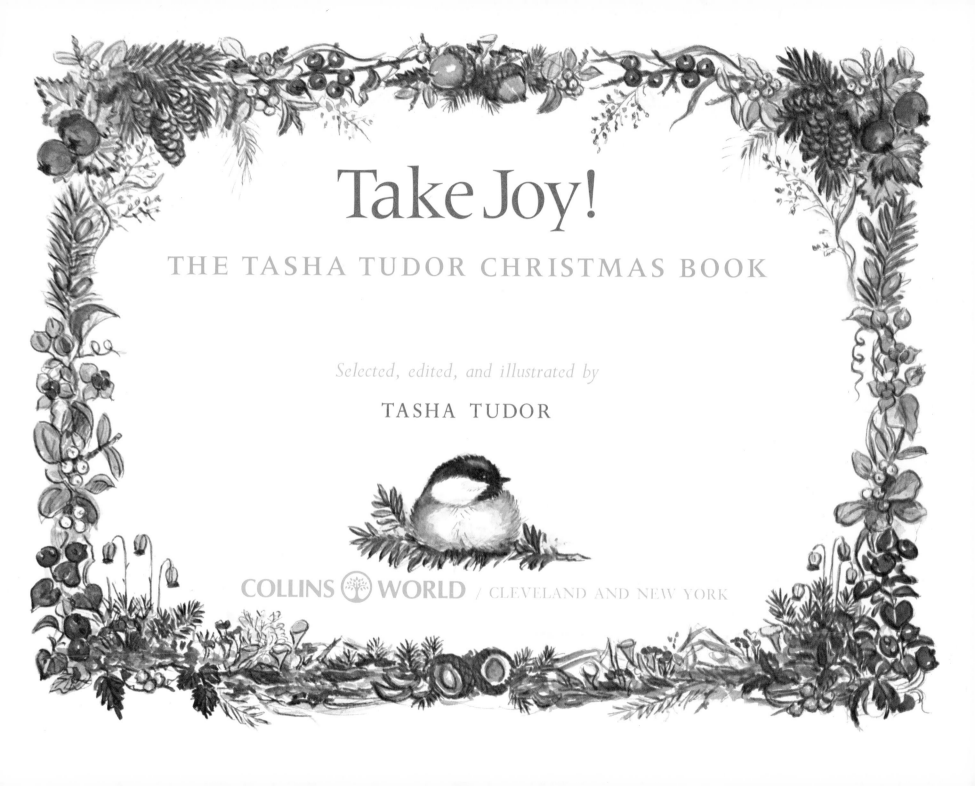

Take Joy!

THE TASHA TUDOR CHRISTMAS BOOK

Selected, edited, and illustrated by

TASHA TUDOR

COLLINS WORLD / CLEVELAND AND NEW YORK

COPYRIGHT ACKNOWLEDGEMENTS

The editor and The World Publishing Company herewith render thanks to the following authors, publishers, and agents whose interest, co-operation, and permission to reprint have made possible the preparation of *Take Joy: The Tasha Tudor Christmas Book*. All possible care has been taken to trace the ownership of every selection included and to make full acknowledgement for its use. If any errors have accidentally occurred, they will be corrected in subsequent editions, provided notification is sent to the publishers.

Charles Scribner's Sons, for "To His Saviour, a Child, a Present by a Child" by Robert Herrick. Reprinted by permission of Charles Scribner's Sons.

Columbia University Press, for "Noel Sing We" from *Early English Christmas Carols* edited by Rossell H. Robbins. Reprinted by permission of Columbia University Press.

D. E. Collins and Messrs. J. M. Dent and Sons, Ltd., and Dodd, Mead and Co., for "A Christmas Carol" by G. K. Chesterton from *The Wild Knight and Other Poems*. Reprinted by permission of D. E. Collins, Messrs. J. M. Dent and Sons, Ltd., and Dodd, Mead and Co.

Doubleday & Company, Inc., for "The Gift of the Magi" from *The Four Million* by O. Henry. Reprinted by permission of Doubleday & Company, Inc.

Flensted Publishers, for R. P. Keigwin's translation of "The Fir Tree" by Hans Christian Andersen. Reprinted by permission of Flensted Publishers, Odense, Denmark.

Harper & Row, Publishers, Inc., for "The Caravan" from *This Way to Christmas* by Ruth Sawyer, copyright 1916 by Harper & Row, Publishers, Inc. Renewal, 1944, by Ruth Sawyer Durand. Reprinted by permission of Harper & Row, Publishers, Inc.

Harry and Eleanor Farjeon, for their poem "Our Brother is Born." Reprinted by permission of the authors.

The Macmillan Company, for "Christmas in London" from *Little Dog Toby* by Rachel Field, copyright 1928 by The Macmillan Company. Reprinted by permission of The Macmillan Company.

New Directions Publishing Corporation, J. M. Dent and Sons, Ltd., and the Literary Executors of the Dylan Thomas Estate, for an excerpt from *A Child's Christmas in Wales* by Dylan Thomas, copyright 1954 by New Directions. Reprinted by permission of the publishers, New Directions Publishing Corporation, J. M. Dent and Sons, Ltd., and the Literary Executors of the Dylan Thomas Estate.

Nora Burglon, for "The Christmas Coin." Reprinted by permission of the author.

Schmitt, Hall & McCreary Company, publishers, for "Here We Come A-Caroling" arranged by Torstein O. Kvamme from *The Christmas Caroler's Book in Song and Story*. Reprinted by permission of Schmitt, Hall & McCreary Company, Minneapolis, Minnesota.

The World Publishing Company, for "The Twelve Days of Christmas" from *Best Loved Songs and Hymns* edited by James Morehead and Albert Morehead, copyright 1965 by James Morehead. Reprinted by permission of The World Publishing Company.

The author also wishes to thank Wendy Worth and Joan Knight for their help in preparing this volume.

Published by Wm. Collins + World Publishing Co., Inc.
2080 W. 117th St., Cleveland, Ohio 44111
Published simultaneously in Canada by
Nelson, Foster & Scott Ltd.
Library of Congress catalog card number: AC 66–10645
ISBN # (Trade) 0-529-04962-7
Library 0-529-00208-6
NE66
Text copyright © 1966 by The World Publishing Company
Illustrations copyright © 1966 by Tasha Tudor
Designed by Jack Jaget

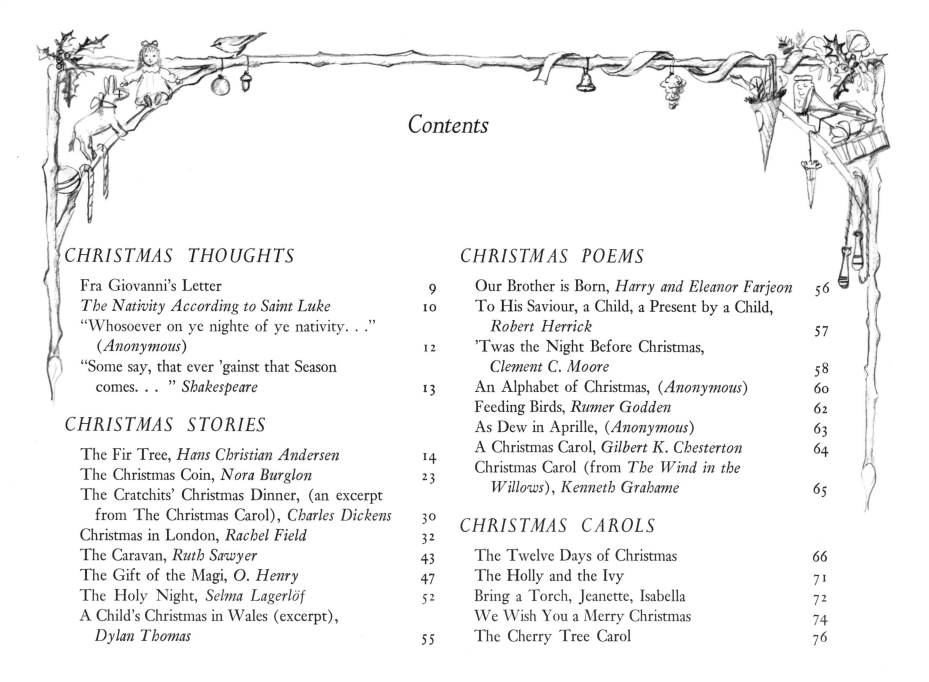

Contents

CHRISTMAS LORE AND LEGENDS

TASHA TUDOR'S CHRISTMAS

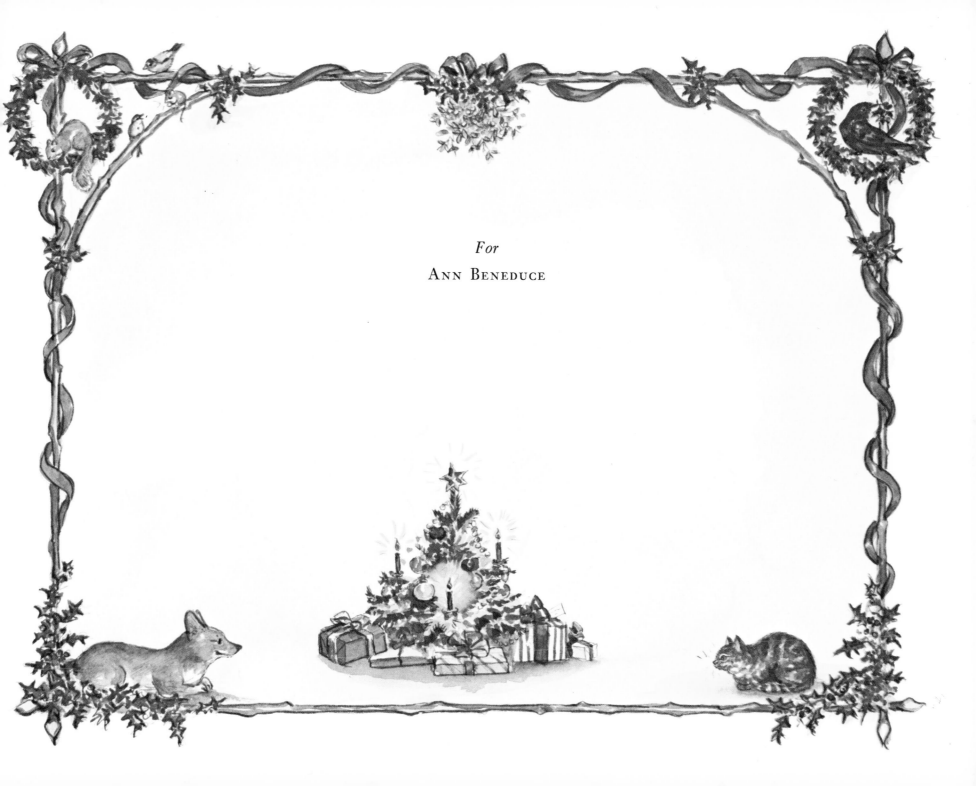

For

ANN BENEDUCE

Take Joy!

I SALUTE YOU! There is nothing I can give you which you have not; but there is much, that, while I cannot give, you can take.

No heaven can come to us unless our hearts find rest in it today. Take Heaven.

No peace lies in the future which is not hidden in this present instant. Take Peace.

The gloom of the world is but a shadow; behind it, yet, within our reach, is joy. Take Joy.

And so, at this Christmas time, I greet you, with the prayer that for you, now and forever, the day breaks and the shadows flee away.

FRA GIOVANNI

A.D. 1513

And it came to pass in those days that there went out a decree from Caesar Augustus that all the world should be taxed. And all went to be taxed, every one into his own city. And Joseph also went up from Galilee, out of the city of Nazareth, into Judea, unto the city of David, which is called Bethlehem (because he was of the

house and lineage of David), to be
taxed with Mary his espoused wife,
being great with child.
And so it was, that, while they
were there, the days were accomplish-
ed that she should be delivered. And
she brought forth her firstborn son,
and wrapped him in swaddling clothes
and laid him in a manger; because
there was no room for them in the inn.
And there were in the same country
shepherds abiding in the fields,
keeping watch over their flocks by night.
And, lo, the angel of the Lord came
upon them, and the glory of the
Lord shone round about them; and
they were sore afraid.

And the angel said unto them,
Fear not; for behold, I bring you
good tidings of great joy, which
shall be to all people. For unto
you is born this day in the city of
David a Saviour, which is
Christ the Lord. And this
shall be a sign unto you; Ye shall
find the babe wrapped in swaddling
clothes, lying in a manger.
And suddenly there was with
the angel a multitude of heavenly
host praising God, and saying,
Glory to God in the highest, and
on earth peace, good will toward
men.

the Christmas Story according to St. Luke

12

"*Whosoever on ye nighte of ye nativity . . .*"

"WHOSOEVER on ye nighte of ye nativity of ye younge Lord Jesus, in ye greate snows, shall fare forth bearing a succulent bone for ye lost and lamenting hounde, a whisp of hay for ye shivering horse, a cloak of warm raiment for ye stranded wayfarer, . . . a garland of bright berries for one who has worn chains, a dish of crumbs for all huddled birds who thought that song was dead, and divers lush sweetmeats for such babes' faces as peer from lonely windows,

To him shall be proffered and returned gifts of such an astonishment as will rival the hues of the peacock and the harmonies of heaven, so that though he live to ye greate age when man goes stooping and querulous because of the nothing that is left in him, yet shall he walk upright and remembering, as one whose hearte shines like a greate star in his breaste."

ANONYMOUS

Christmastide

Some say that ever 'gainst that season comes
Wherein our Saviour's birth is celebrated,
The bird of dawning singeth all night long;
And then, they say, no spirit can walk abroad;
The nights are wholesome; then no planets strike,
No fairy takes, nor witch hath power to charm,
So hallow'd and so gracious is the time.

WILLIAM SHAKESPEARE
Hamlet, Act I, Scene I

The Fir Tree

HANS CHRISTIAN ANDERSEN

Out in the wood was a fir tree, such a pretty little fir tree. It had a good place to grow in and all the air and sunshine it wanted, while all around it were numbers of bigger comrades, both firs and pines. But the little fir tree was in such a passionate hurry to grow. It paid no heed to the warmth of the sun or the sweetness of the air, and it took no notice of the village children who went chattering along when they were out after strawberries or raspberries; sometimes they came there with a whole jugful or had strawberries threaded on a straw, and then they sat down by the little tree and said, "Oh, what a dear little tree!" That was not at all the kind of thing the tree wanted to hear.

The next year it had shot up a good deal, and the year after that its girth had grown even bigger; for, with a fir tree, you can always tell how old it is by the number of rings it has.

"Oh, if only I were a tall tree like the others," sighed the little fir. "Then I'd be able to spread out my branches all 'round me and see out over the wide world with my top. The birds would come and nest in my branches and, whenever it was windy, I'd be able to nod grandly."

It took no pleasure in the sunshine or the birds or the pink clouds that, morning and evening, went sailing overhead.

When winter came and the snow lay sparkling white all around, then a hare would often come bounding along and jump right over the little tree—oh, how annoying that was! . . . But two winters passed and by the third winter the tree had grow so tall that the hare had to run around it. Yes, grow, grow, become tall and old—that was much the finest thing in the world, thought the tree.

In the autumn the woodcutters always came and felled some of the tallest trees. That used to happen every year; and the young fir, which was now quite a sizable tree, trembled at the sight, for the splendid great trees would crack and crash to the ground; their branches were lopped off, and they looked all naked and spindly—they were hardly recognizable—and then they were loaded onto wagons and carted away by horses out of the wood.

Where were they off to? What was in store for them?

In the spring, when the swallow and the stork arrived, the tree asked them, "Do you know where they've gone—where they've been taken to? Have you seen anything of them?"

The swallows knew nothing, but the stork looked thoughtful and replied with a nod, "Yes, I believe I know. I came across a lot of new ships, as I flew here from Egypt; they had splendid masts—I daresay it was they—I could smell the fir, and they asked to be remembered to you. Oh, how straight they stand!"

"How I do wish that I were big enough to fly across the sea! And, as a matter of fact, what sort of a thing is this sea? What does it look like?"

"That would take far too long to explain," said the stork and went his way.

"Rejoice in your youth," said the sunbeams; "rejoice in your lusty growth, and in the young life that is in you." And the wind kissed the tree, and the dew wept tears over it, but this meant nothing to the fir tree.

As Christmas drew near, quite young trees were cut down, trees that often were nothing like so big or so old as our fir tree, which knew no peace and was always longing to get away. These young trees—and they were just the very handsomest ones—always kept their branches; they were laid on wagons and carted away by horses out of the wood.

"Where are they off to?" asked the fir tree. "They are no bigger than I am; there was even one that was much smaller. Why did they all keep their branches? Where are they going?"

"We know, we know!" twittered the sparrows. "We've been peeping in at the windows down in the town; we know where they're going. All the glory and splendor you can imagine awaits them. We looked in through the windowpanes and saw how the trees were planted in the middle of a cozy room and decorated with the loveliest things: gilded apples, honey cakes, toys, and hundreds of candles."

"And then?" asked the fir tree, quivering in every branch. "And then? What happens then?"

"Well, we didn't see any more. But it was magnificent."

"I wonder if it will be my fate to go that dazzling road," cried the tree in delight. "It's even better than crossing the ocean. How I'm longing for Christmas! I'm now just as tall and spreading as the others who were taken away last year. Oh, if only I were already on the wagon—if only I were in the cozy room amidst all that glory and splendor! And then? Yes, there must be something still better, still more beautiful in store for me—or why should they decorate me like that?—something much greater, and much more splendid. But what? Oh, the laboring and longing I go through! I don't know myself what's the matter with me."

"Rejoice in me," said the air and the sunlight; "rejoice in your lusty youth out here in the open."

But the fir tree did nothing of the kind. It went on growing and growing; there it was, winter and summer, always green—dark green. People who saw it remarked, "That's a pretty tree." And at the next Christmastime it was the first to be felled. The axe cut deep through pith and marrow, and the tree fell to the earth with a sigh, faint with pain, with no more thoughts of any happiness; it was so sad at parting from its home, from the place where it had grown up. For it knew that never again would it see those dear old friends, the little bushes and flowers that grew around—yes, and perhaps not even the birds. There was nothing pleasant about such a parting.

The tree didn't come to itself till it was being unloaded in the yard with the other trees and it heard a man say, "That one's a beauty—that's the one we'll have."

Now came two lackeys in full fig and carried the fir tree into a splendid great room. There were portraits all 'round on the walls, and by the big tile fireplace stood huge Chinese vases with lions on their lids. There were rocking-chairs, silk-covered sofas, large tables piled with picture books, and toys worth hundreds of dollars—at least, so said the children. And the fir tree was propped up in a great wooden barrel filled with sand, though no one could see it was a barrel because it was draped 'round with green cloth and was standing on a gay colored carpet. How the tree trembled! Whatever was going to happen? Servants and young ladies alike were soon busy decorating it. On the branches they hung the little nets that had been cut out of colored paper, each net being filled with sweets; gilded apples and walnuts hung down as if they were growing there, and over a hundred red, blue, and white candles were fastened to the branches. Dolls that looked just like living people—such as the tree had never seen before—hovered among the greenery, while right up at the very top they had put a great star of gold tinsel; it was magnificent—you never saw anything like it.

"Tonight," they all said, "tonight it's going to sparkle—you see!"

"Oh, if only tonight were here!" thought the tree. "If only the candles were already lighted! What happens then, I wonder? Do trees come from the wood to look at me? Will the sparrows fly to the window-panes? Shall I take root here and keep my decorations winter and summer?"

Well, well,—a nice lot the fir tree knew! But it had got barkache from sheer longing, and barkache is just as bad for a tree as headache is for the rest of us.

At last the candles were lighted—what a blaze, what magnificence! It made the tree tremble in every branch, until one of the candles set fire to the greenery—didn't that smart!

"Oh dear!" cried the young ladies and quickly put out the fire. The tree was afraid of losing any of its finery, and it felt quite dazed by all that magnificence . . . Then suddenly both folding doors flew open, and a flock of children came tearing in, as if they were going to upset the whole tree. The older people followed soberly behind; the little ones stood quite silent—but only for a moment—then they made the air ring with their shouts of delight.

They danced round the tree, and one present after another was pulled off it. "Whatever are they doing?" thought the tree. "What's going to happen?" The candles burned right down to their branches and, as they did so, they were put out, and the children were allowed to plunder the tree. They rushed in at it, till it creaked in every branch; if it hadn't been fastened to the ceiling by the top and the gold star, it would have tumbled right over.

The children danced around with their splendid toys, and nobody looked at the tree except the old nurse, who went peering among the branches—though this was only to see if there wasn't some fig or apple that had been overlooked.

"A story—tell us a story!" cried the children, dragging a little fat man over towards the tree. He sat down right under it, "for then we are in the greenwood," he said, "and it will be so good for the tree to listen with you. But I'll only tell one story. Would you like the one about Hickory-Dickory or the one about Humpty-Dumpty, who fell downstairs and yet came to the throne and married the Princess?"

"Hickory-Dickory," cried some; "Humpty-Dumpty," cried others. There was such yelling and shouting; only the fir tree was quite silent and thought "Shan't I be in it as well? Isn't there anything for me to do?" But of course it *had* been in it—it had done just what it had to do.

The little fat man told them the story of Humpty-Dumpty, who fell downstairs and yet came to the throne and married the Princess. And the children clapped their hands and called out, "Tell us another story! One more!"

They wanted to have Hickory-Dickory as well, but they only got the one about Humpty-Dumpty. The fir tree stood there in silent thought; never had the birds out in the wood told a story like that. "Humpty-Dumpty fell downstairs and yet married the Princess—well, well, that's how they go on in the great world!" thought the fir tree, and felt it must all be true, because the storyteller was such a nice man. "Well, who knows? Maybe I too shall fall downstairs and marry a Princess." And it looked forward to being decked out again next day with candles and toys, tinsel and fruit.

"I shan't tremble tomorrow," it thought. "I mean to enjoy my magnificence to the full. Tomorrow I shall again hear the story about Humpty-Dumpty and perhaps the one about Hickory-Dickory as well." And the tree stood the whole night in silent thought.

The next morning in came a manservant and a maid. "Now all the doings will begin again," thought the tree. Instead, they hauled it out of the room, up the stairs and into the attic, where they stowed it away in a dark corner out of the daylight. "What's the meaning of this?" wondered the tree. "What is there for me to do here? What am I to listen to?" And it leaned up against the wall and stood there thinking and thinking . . . It had plenty of time for that, because days and nights went by. No one came up there, and when at last somebody did come it was to put some big boxes away in the corner; the tree was completely hidden—you might have thought it was utterly forgotten.

"It's winter by now outside," thought the tree. "The

ground will be hard and covered with snow, people wouldn't be able to plant me; so I expect I shall have to shelter here till the spring. How considerate! How kind people are! . . . If only it weren't so dark and so terribly lonely in here! Not even a little hare . . . It was so jolly out in the wood, when the snow was lying and the hare went bounding past; yes, even when it jumped right over me, though I didn't like it at the time. Up here it's too lonely for words."

"Peep-peep!" squeaked a little mouse just then, creeping out on the floor; and another one followed it. They sniffed at the fir tree and slipped in and out of its branches. "It's horribly cold," said the little mice, "though this is actually a splendid place to be in, don't you think, old fir tree?"

"I'm not a bit old," answered the fir tree. "There are lots of people who are much older than I am."

"Where do you hail from?" asked the mice, "and what do you know?" (They were being dreadfully inquisitive). "Do tell us about the loveliest place on earth. Have you ever been there? Have you been in the larder, where there are cheeses on the shelves and hams hanging from the ceiling—where you can dance on tallow candles and you go in thin and come out fat?"

"No, I don't know the larder," said the tree, "but I know the wood, where the sun shines and the birds sing"; and then it told all about the days when it was young. The little mice had never heard anything like it before, and they listened closely and said, "Why, what a lot you've seen! How happy you must have been!"

"I?" said the fir tree and pondered over what it had just been saying. "Yes, they were really very pleasant times." But then it went on to tell them about Christmas Eve, when it had been tricked out with cakes and candles.

"Ooh!" said the little mice. "You *have* been a happy old fir tree."

"I'm not a bit old," repeated the tree; "I've only this winter come from the wood. I'm just in my prime; my growth is only being checked for a while."

"What lovely stories you tell!" said the little mice; and they came back the following night with four more little mice who wanted to hear the tree tell stories, and the more it told the better it remembered everything itself, thinking, "Those were really rather jolly times. But they may come again, they may come again. Humpty-Dumpty fell downstairs and yet won the Princess; perhaps I too may win a Princess." And then the fir tree suddenly remembered such a sweet little birch tree growing out in the wood; that, for the fir tree, would be a really beautiful Princess.

"Who is Humpty-Dumpty?" asked the little mice. Then the fir tree told them the whole fairy tale; it could remember every word; and the little mice were ready to jump up to the top of the tree for sheer enjoyment. The night after, many more mice turned up and, on the Sunday, even two rats. But these declared that the tale was not at all amusing, which disappointed the little mice because now they didn't think so much of it either.

"Is that the only story you know?" asked the rats.

"Only that one," replied the tree. "I heard it on the happiest evening of my life, but I never realized then how happy I was."

"It's a fearfully dull story. Don't you know any about pork and tallow candles? One about the larder?"

"No," said the tree.

"Well, then, thank you for nothing," answered the rats and went home again.

In the end, the little mice kept away as well, and the tree said with a sigh, "It really was rather nice with them sitting round me, those eager little mice, listening to what I told them. Now that's over too . . . though I shall remember to enjoy myself, when I'm taken out again."

But when would that happen? Well, it happened one morning when people came up and rummaged about the attic. The boxes were being moved, and the tree was dragged out. They certainly dumped it rather hard onto the floor, but one of the men at once pulled it along towards the stairs where there was daylight.

"Life's beginning again for me!" thought the tree. It could feel the fresh air, the first sunbeams—and now it was out in the courtyard. Everything happened so quickly that the tree quite forgot to look at itself, there was so much to see all around. The yard gave onto a garden where everything was in bloom. The roses smelled so sweet and fresh as they hung over the little trellis, and the lime trees were blossoming, and the swallows flew around saying, "Kvirra-virra-veet, my husband's arrived!" But it wasn't the fir tree they were thinking of.

"This is the life for me!" it cried out joyfully, spreading out its branches. Alas! they were all withered and yellow, and the tree lay in a corner among weeds and nettles. The gold paper star was still in its place at the top and glittered away in the bright sunshine.

Playing in the courtyard itself were a few of the merry children who at Christmastime had danced round the tree and were so pleased with it. One of the smallest ran up and tore off the gold star.

"Look what I've found still there on that nasty old Christmas tree!" he said, trampling on the branches so that they crackled under his boots.

And the tree looked at the fresh beauty of the flowers in the garden, and then at itself, and it wished it had stayed in that dark corner up in the attic. It thought of the fresh days of its youth in the wood, of that merry Christmas Eve, and of the little mice who had listened with such delight to the story of Humpty-Dumpty.

"All over!" said the poor tree, "if only I had been happy while I could! All over!"

And the man came and chopped up the tree into small pieces, till there was quite a heap. It made a fine blaze under the big copper pot in the fireplace; and the tree groaned so loudly that every groan was like a little shot going off. This made the children who were playing run in and sit down before the fire; and as they looked into it they shouted "bang!"—but at every pop (which was a deep groan) the tree thought of a summer's day in the wood, or of a winter's night out there when the stars were shining; it thought of Christmas Eve and of Humpty-Dumpty, the only fairy tale it had ever heard and was able to tell . . . And finally the tree was burned right up.

The boys were playing in the yard, and the smallest of them had on his chest the gold star which had crowned the tree on its happiest evening. That was all over now, and it was all over with the tree, and so it is with the story. That's what happens at last to every story—all over, all over!

The Christmas Coin

NORA BURGLON

THE SUN was setting. One might truthfully say that it was Christmas Eve at last. To Nicolina and Guldklumpen it had been a long time arriving; but so it always was with days that amounted to anything.

"Now," Guldklumpen declared, "that we have set up the big Christmas sheaf for our birds' Yule feast, don't you think it only just and proper to set up a sheaf for the tomte man's birds also?"

Nicolina stared at her brother in surprise. "The tomte man's birds?" she echoed, "why I never heard that he had any."

"Silly," cried Guldklumpen, "how do you suppose the good elf can see and hear so much if it isn't the birds that tell him?"

When Nicolina heard that she was all for helping to get a sheaf together to hang before the house of the tomte. Small wonder, too. Folks always tried to please the little elf if they were fortunate enough to have one on the place. As long as he remained at a farm he dragged good luck from all the other places in the valley. Indeed, a tomte farm always had the fattest cows, and the biggest horses and the smartest children in the whole settlement. However, if folks did not treat him kindly it was known more times than once, that he had carried off all the luck he ever brought here, and even more, when the truth was told.

That is the reason matters had gone so badly at Malmostrand the first years that Guldklumpen and Nicolina lived there. Some one owned it before who had so little sense that he had not even put out a Christmas porridge for the little man. Small wonder he had left Malmostrand. It was not until Guldklumpen carried up an old sea chest from the strand and built him a very fine house against the south wall of the goat house that he came back, and Malmostrand became a real "gård" again.

To make his place so much better this Christmas, Nicolina and Guldklumpen had set up a little forest of fir trees about his house and had planted a spruce tree right before the door, on which they had hung hand hammered nails that tinkled like fairy bells in the wind. Nicolina had hung some paper stars upon it too, but those the wind had blown away.

Guldklumpen said he thought it would be best to tie the tomte man's sheaf about the worn end of the old broom. Since they had so few stalks left it would make the sheaf look so much bigger. It went exactly as Guld-klumpen said. The sheaf became so fine looking that the two had to sit down on the old stone boat and stare at it a full minute. "Do you know that mother already has his Yule porridge ready for him?" whispered Nicolina.

That reminded them they had not yet told the goats what day tomorrow was, so the two of them flew out into the stable and told them tomorrow was Yule. That would give them something to look forward to, for of course every living thing on the "gard" had to have a taste of the good Yule food on Christmas day.

That done the two of them dragged the heavy iron caldron inside and filled it to the brim with snow. They, as well as the rest of Scandinavia, must have their Yule baths tonight for no one was so stupid that he scrubbed his house from ceiling to floor and forgot to take a bath himself.

After the two had hauled the caldron in Nicolina gave a heavy sigh, "Well, now that we have done that, what do we do next?"

Guldklumpen sat upon the stoop and made crooked figures in the snow. "I know," he said brightly, "let's take some of our bread cakes over to Stina Mor. When folks

get to be as old as she, people seldom think of them even at the Yule time of the year."

"The very thing to do," cried Nicolina, so the two of them flew into the house and picked out some of their best bread cakes and sugar plums for Stina Mor.

It was the custom in Sweden for folks as old as Guldklumpen and Nicolina to go Yule calling at Christmastime. Any one knew that when callers opened the door and said "Happy Yule" at Christmastime it was only proper that one should come forth with a bread cake or two. Nicolina and Guldklumpen had not only said a happy Yule, they had also said a fortunate New Year. For that reason they had gathered up so many Yule cakes that they had a great heap under the red wooden candlestick on the middle of the table.

Before the two of them tied up Stina Mor's bag they counted the cakes once more. It always made one's blessings seem bigger when one counted them more than once, especially when they were blessings like Yule cakes and sugar plums.

It gave the two a feeling of importance to walk up to that faded gate today and push it open. So much snow was lodged against it that it did not even squeak as it always did in the summer. Therefore it was a complete surprise to Stina Mor when the scraping came upon the stoop.

"Is some one there?" she said, and her voice sounded strangely eager, as if she had been expecting somebody. "Who is it?" she asked as the door opened, for the years she had lived and the tears she had shed for a son who had gone away never to return had dimmed Stina Mor's eyes.

"Guldklumpen and Nicolina," said the two. "We have come to wish you a happy Yule and to leave a few cakes and sugar plums with you."

"God bless you," said Stina Mor, "for thinking of an old woman. But you must know that the wants of the flesh are few when one gets as old as I. It is the craving of the soul that eats the heart away."

Guldklumpen nodded understandingly to his sister. Stina Mor always talked so when she was speaking of that son of hers.

"It is ten years since he went away. I thought perhaps he would come home this Christmas," she said, and her voice trailed off into nothingness. Then after a little she said, "Perhaps the reason he doesn't come is because he can't find me. I've had to move so often, and before long I suppose I'll have to move again." Stina Mor said this as if she were talking to herself, but Nicolina guessed that she meant she would have to move over to the Old People's Home. The mother had said her eyes were becoming so dim she could not take care of herself much longer. Nicolina imagined that the old lady did not want to leave her home; for, as she said that, she sighed just as if it were not Christmas Eve at all. After a little she continued, "I wouldn't care, though, if I might only see Daki once more."

The children felt that Stina Mor was speaking more to herself than to them, and it was not long before Nicolina said: "Well, we must be going home now. Mother is waiting for us, since it is Christmas Eve."

"Christmas Eve. Yes, so it is. Now just wait a moment," said Stina Mor, getting up from her chair and fumbling about in the cupboard.

"Here," she said, "here is a twenty-five-öre piece. That is my Christmas gift to you."

"No, Stina Mor," said Nicolina, "you must not give us anything."

"You *must* take my gift," said the other. "It is Christmas money and for that reason it has a very special blessing."

After thanking Stina Mor, and again wishing her a happy Christmas, the two softly closed the door behind them and set out for home; but somehow they did not feel so much like Christmas now as they had when they first decided to give their offerings to Stina Mor. Perhaps it was because they had accepted the twenty-five-öre piece when they knew that Stina Mor needed it so much herself.

Both Nicolina and Guldklumpen were busy with their own thoughts, so they trudged on in silence. Each was wondering how it would be possible for Stina Mor ever to find that lost son of hers. "If only he would come home just this one Christmas!" said Nicolina.

Guldklumpen shook his head. Perhaps he was thinking of what the folk had said in the village—that he was only a useless fellow who had long since forgotten his old mother.

It was dark when the two reached home, and the moon had just climbed atop Stina Mor's little hut when the two of them stepped into Olina's little cottage; but instead of the mother they found a note which said that she had gone over to Magda's place. The baby wasn't feeling well.

Guldklumpen shook his head. "That is just like that baby," he said. "He screams in church when the minister preaches, and he yells so that Magda has to take him along wherever she goes, and now he has to get sick on Christmas Eve."

Nicolina said nothing. She was busy. This was Doppare Dagen, the day when one dipped one's bread into the broth of the kettle without first dishing it up into a bowl. Nicolina got a couple of pieces of hard bread out of the cupboard while Guldklumpen climbed on top of the high stool and dropped the twenty-five-öre piece into the silver teapot. It made a big tinkle. That was because the silver teapot was empty. "We will have to do something very special with that money," said Guldklumpen, "because Stina Mor said it had a very special blessing."

Nicolina had no opportunity to make a reply, for at that very moment there came a rap upon the door. It was a strange rap—not at all as if the person had ever stood upon their stoop before.

Since Guldklumpen was the head of the house when the mother was not at home, he went to the door and opened it.

A strange man stood without. "Have you a crust to share with a stranger?" he asked. "I have come a great distance, and I am both weary and hungry."

The rest of the year one might do as one wished, but at Christmastime not a soul might be turned away from any door in Scandinavia; so Nicolina and Guldklumpen did exactly as they had been taught when they invited the stranger in and asked him to sit down at the table while a bowl of broth was fetched for him.

While he was eating, the children withdrew to the *spis* to whisper to each other. "He looks as if he is very poor," said Nicolina; "his clothes are so worn."

"Perhaps it is because he has come from far away," said Guldklumpen.

Nicolina looked at the man again and shook her head. "I've been thinking," she said. "It is about Stina Mor."

It was only natural that one should think about Stina Mor when one saw a traveler, for had she not been sitting there by her window until her eyes became dim waiting for just such a person?

"If the man is as poor as he looks, perhaps we could get him to play that he is Stina Mor's son just for tonight," suggested Nicolina. "We could give him the twenty-five-öre piece."

Guldklumpen looked at his sister. "But would that be right?" he demanded.

"It would be just as right as playing there is a Yule-elf that brings the Christmas gifts, when there really is none at all," replied Nicolina. "Besides, he has no one, just as Stina Mor hasn't. Perhaps they will both be made happy."

"Well, we can ask him," Guldklumpen agreed, but since he was not so fully acquainted with the plan as Nicolina, it was she who had to do the talking this time.

The man looked at them curiously. For a long time he sat there as if he had not heard. Then he said, "Stina Mor," aloud, as if he had known the name before and forgotten it and now was learning it again.

"Stina Mor said that money had a special blessing on account of its being Christmas money," said Nicolina. "Perhaps it will make you lucky."

"It has already made me lucky," he said, and got up as if he were ready to leave that very moment.

"Wait," said Nicolina. "Wait until I get the twenty-five-öre piece out of the silver teapot."

"No. I really do not need the money at all now that I've had such a good bowl of broth," said he. "But I'll play the game with you," he added, "if you will show me how to get to Stina Mor's house."

"But you must take the money," said Nicolina, "because you need special blessings, and we have blessings enough as it is." With that she put the coin in the stranger's hand. Meanwhile Guldklumpen had got into his outdoor clothing. He would go with the stranger part of the way lest he miss the path. Nicolina, after considering a moment, decided to go, too. When one sent a stranger upon an errand as important as making Stina Mor happy, it was best to go along and see that it was done right.

Nicolina and Guldklumpen had much to talk about as they skimmed along the path upon their short, forest skis, but the stranger who had come to them that night had not a word to say. It was almost as if he walked along whispering a prayer to himself; for now and then his lips moved, but there were no words.

The night was still and beautiful, and the snow glittered like stars in a white sky. Nicolina commenced to sing *Silent Night, Peaceful Night,* and Guldklumpen joined her. The two of them could not help wondering about the stranger as they sang their song. Perhaps he, too, had a mother he had not gone home to see for many years.

"We will not go along inside," said Nicolina, when they reached the hut, "but we are going to look in through the window to see that you do it right." It was best to tell the man so that he would understand just how important was this matter of making Stina Mor happy.

"No, it is best you come along inside," he said, as if he found it difficult to say even those few words.

The old lady was sitting by the fire as if still waiting for that rap she had hoped for these many years. When it came she sprang to her feet and cried, "It is he. He has come at last." In a moment she had her arms about him. "Daki," she screamed, "my boy."

"Mother," he said, and there were tears in his eyes, "Mother, I thought that I would never find you." Then he turned to Guldklumpen and Nicolina. "Had it not been for these two young people," he said, "I should have wandered by without finding you." Then he told a strange tale of years in the tropics, shipwreck and fever. "Since you had moved away from the old home, my letters did not reach you, and so I have wandered from one place to the other looking for you, until tonight," and he stretched out an eager hand towards Nicolina and Guldklumpen as if he wished to draw them into the warm glow of the fire, beside the little mother they all loved.

"No, we must be going, now," said Nicolina. "It is Christmas Eve, and our mother will be home." So, wishing them both a happy Christmas, the children set off across the fields.

"Didn't that turn out exactly like a fairy story?" demanded Guldklumpen when the two of them were outside.

"It was that Christmas coin Stina Mor gave us which brought all that blessing," said the sister, and she thrust her hand into her pocket as if she still could feel it there.

Then she gave a cry and stopped stock-still. Out came her hand, and there were two shining coins.

"Why, Guldklumpen, look here!" she cried. "I have two coins in my pocket!"

And at the same time her brother brought two out of his own pocket. "Do you suppose the man put them there?" cried Nicolina.

"It might have been the Yule tomte!" said Guldklumpen. "One never knows what may happen at this time of year!"

The Cratchits' Christmas Dinner

CHARLES DICKENS

Such a bustle ensued that you might have thought a goose the rarest of all birds; a feathered phenomenon, to which a black swan was a matter of course—and in truth it was something very like it in that house. Mrs. Cratchit made the gravy (ready beforehand in a little saucepan) hissing hot; Master Peter mashed the potatoes with incredible vigor; Miss Belinda sweetened up the apple-sauce; Martha dusted the hot plates; Bob took Tiny Tim beside him in a tiny corner at the table; the two young Cratchits set chairs for everybody, not forgetting themselves, and mounting guard upon their posts, crammed spoons into their mouths, lest they should shriek for goose before their turn came to be helped. At last the dishes were set on, and grace was said. It was succeeded by a breathless pause, as Mrs. Cratchit, looking slowly all along the

H IS ACTIVE little crutch was heard upon the floor, and back came Tiny Tim before another word was spoken, escorted by his brother and sister to his stool before the fire; and while Bob, turning up his cuffs—as if, poor fellow, they were capable of being made more shabby—compounded some hot mixture in a jug with gin and lemons, and stirred it round and round and put it on the hob to simmer; Master Peter, and the two ubiquitous young Cratchits went to fetch the goose, with which they soon returned in high procession.

carving-knife, prepared to plunge it in the breast; but when she did, and when the long-expected gush of stuffing issued forth, one murmur of delight arose all round the board, and even Tiny Tim, excited by the two young Cratchits, beat on the table with the handle of his knife, and feebly cried Hurrah!

There never was such a goose. Bob said he didn't believe there ever was such a goose cooked. Its tenderness and flavor, size and cheapness, were the themes of universal admiration. Eked out by apple-sauce and mashed potatoes, it was a sufficient dinner for the whole family; indeed, as Mrs. Cratchit said with great delight (surveying one small atom of a bone upon the dish), they hadn't ate it all at last! Yet every one had had enough, and the youngest Cratchits in particular, were steeped in sage and onion to the eyebrows! But now, the plates being changed by Miss Belinda, Mrs. Cratchit left the room alone—too nervous to bear witness—to take the pudding up and bring it in.

Suppose it should not be done enough! Suppose it should break in turning out! Suppose somebody should have got over the wall of the back-yard, and stolen it, while they were merry with goose—a supposition at which the two young Cratchits became livid! All sorts of horrors were supposed.

Hallo! A great deal of steam! The pudding was out of the copper. A smell like a washing-day! That was the cloth. A smell like an eating-house and a pastrycook's next door to each other, with a laundress's next door to that! That was the pudding! In half a minute Mrs. Cratchit entered—flushed, but smiling proudly—with the pudding, like a speckled cannon-ball, so hard and firm, blazing in half of half-a-quartern of ignited brandy, and bedight with Christmas holly stuck into the top.

Oh, a wonderful pudding! Bob Cratchit said, and calmly too, that he regarded it as the greatest success achieved by Mrs. Cratchit since their marriage. Mrs. Cratchit said that now the weight was off her mind, she would confess she had had her doubts about the quantity of flour. Everybody had something to say about it, but nobody said or thought it was at all a small pudding for a large family. It would have been flat heresy to do so. Any Cratchit would have blushed to hint at such a thing.

At last the dinner was all done, the cloth was cleared, the hearth swept, and the fire made up. The compound in the jug being tasted, and considered perfect, apples and oranges were put upon the table, and a shovelful of chestnuts on the fire. Then all the Cratchit family drew round the hearth, in what Bob Cratchit called a circle, meaning half a one; and at Bob Cratchit's elbow stood the family display of glass. Two tumblers, and a custard-cup without a handle.

These held the hot stuff from the jug, however, as well as golden goblets would have done; and Bob served it out with beaming looks, while the chestnuts on the fire sputtered and cracked noisily. Then Bob proposed:

"A Merry Christmas to us all, my dears. God bless us!" Which all the family re-echoed.

"God bless us every one!" said Tiny Tim, the last of all.

Christmas in London

from Little Dog Toby

RACHEL FIELD

LITTLE DOG TOBY traveled with his master and a Punch and Judy Show. They traveled a great many roads from Land's End to Yorkshire.

Now it was London again and a little room under the gables of an old house in High Holborn. London seemed strange to Toby who had once known its streets so well. He had to begin learning his way about all over again. He wondered more than he had in his earlier days, wondered about the houses and who lived in them; about the shops, what they sold and whether business was good;

most of all he wondered about the people who passed him, where they were going and why.

That week before the holiday the weather turned nipping cold with ice in all the gutters and sometimes sleet that froze as it fell and made the street slippery as glass. The sun set almost before you knew it was up and the hot gingerbread and muffin men did a thriving business at teatime. Street lamps burned early and late, and shop and house windows were bright with flaring gas-jets. Even the poorest tradesmen hung up bunches of holly and mistletoe, or strings of colored mottoes in honor of the season. Streets were a jumble of Christmas trees and greens, of penny-toymen with their trays and crowds of hurrying, bundle-laden people. Toby thought it a very fine time to be up and about even if it was sometimes hard to find space on the pavements to set up the show wagon.

The coppers did not drop into the hat so fast as they had before and there were no sixpences to speak of. People were too busy buying gifts to hang on children's Christmas trees or to put in their stockings.

"Still, h'it's not 'alf bad, eh Toby?" Master would say, blowing on his fingers to limber them up between performances and buttoning Toby tighter into his red plush jacket. He would thump his tail and stare down at all the people hurrying by, with high hopes that he might catch a glimpse of a small white poodle and a mistress in the latest fashion of muff and tippet and shiny topped boots.

The day before Christmas was raw and windy with sudden blinding flurries of snow that made them hurry to take shelter in doorways and under arcades. As they waited in one of these Toby fell into conversation with a Blindman's dog.

"And how is business with you today?" asked the other, who was a shaggy little fellow with a tail like a banner just off the field of battle. "We've tried all the corners from Hyde Park to Saint Paul's, and it's bad, very bad."

"But it might be worse," Toby reminded him. "It might be a fog and then no one would see us at all."

"Ah," said the Blindman's dog, "I see you look on the

bright side of things. So did I when I was your age, but lately what with all these upstarts crowding us off the very pavements, I confess I get a little low in my mind."

"Still, Christmas is Christmas," persisted Toby.

"Well, no one can deny that," admitted the other, "and it only comes once a year."

"And there's always the smell of the evergreen and the pies and the plum puddings in the shops when you go by," added Toby, "and the little boys and girls always *want* to give you pennies even if they have spent all theirs."

"A penny that clinks in your cup is worth two in other people's pockets, though," said the Blindman's dog, with a solemn headshake, as they moved on.

"Merry Christmas just the same," Toby barked after him and followed Master to a place just at the entrance of a large toyshop where he was already setting up the Punch and Judy Show.

They played there all the rest of the day and Toby was careful to watch all the children and dogs who passed. In the times between his own special part he had a fine chance to look over the audience and whoever entered or left the toyshop. It had two big windows, packed full of the most wonderful dolls and wooden animals; Noah's Arks and doll houses; ships and skates and queer carved boxes that played the prettiest tinkling tunes. Whenever the doors opened or shut on customers Toby could hear snatches of music and it made him feel almost like a puppy again, it sounded so gay.

Pennies were still rather scanty. Toby was an artist, however, and went through his part with just as much spirit and as many barks and wags and paw-givings as if business were at its best. The little boys and girls were as delighted as ever over his antics and several of them reached up and gave him bits of their own gingerbread which he ate with pleasure while Mr. Punch and the rest were acting. He liked to see the children go into the toy-shop and come out later on with enormous knobby looking parcels held very tight. Sometimes he could tell what was inside the wrappings; dolls and Noah's Arks were easy. Once he was very much flattered to have a little girl in a shabby dress and shawl lift up a queerly shaped pink plush dog for him to see. She evidently thought it as good as real, and though Toby couldn't honestly feel much enthusiasm for it, he looked down as if he did, and she ran off as pleased and proud as could be.

It must have been about the middle of the afternoon when Toby noticed the Little Boy in kilts and Scotch cap. He was standing alone at the edge of the crowd and Toby thought he had never seen any child enjoy the show quite so much. He laughed and clapped and hopped up and down and he never once took his eyes off Toby. Now Toby was used to this sort of thing by that time, but there was something about this Little Boy that made you notice him. It wasn't just his clothes, though they were handsomer than most of the others. It was the way his blue eyes shone and the set of his head and shoulders when he stood watching with his hands in his pockets.

Toby fairly outdid himself to please the Little Boy and each time he could manage to look his way he saw him squeezing in nearer to the front, his eyes very round and his cap all on one side, with excited interest. Then just as things were going their best and Toby was getting ready for the nose-nipping part, there was a commotion in the crowd. Toby had to keep his mind on business, not to miss any barks or bites, and he dared not look to see what was the matter, but he felt it in his bones that it had something to do with the Little Boy. He was right, for when he was able at last to turn his eyes that way, it was to see a worried looking lady and a tall man in uniform leading him off between them. It was plain from the Little Boy's shoulders and the way he hung back that he did not want to leave the Punch and Judy Show. Indeed Toby could hear his protests even above Mr. Punch's squeakings. Every one was staring after the three in a curious sort of way and the proprietor of the toyshop

stood in the door, bowing long after they had passed out of sight.

Master, of course, saw nothing of all this, being behind the little stage and busy putting the puppets through their paces. He grumbled a good deal when he came out to pass the hat round and found so many people had gone away, and Toby couldn't tell him the reason.

The lamplighters made their rounds early that evening. It was barely teatime and yet it might have been midnight from the darkness and all the lighted windows. People still hurried by jostling each other off the pavements and looking like bumpy gnomes with their mufflers and great-coats and queer-shaped bundles. Snow powdered their caps and shoulders and frosted the stage of the Punch and Judy Show. Toby's paws made little prints in it and

whenever he had to come to the front to do his part his whiskers grew white with the clinging flakes. The plush coat did not seem nearly as warm as usual.

Then, suddenly there was a great clattering of horse's hoofs. A soldier in magnificent scarlet coat and bushy black helmet was reining up beside them. The Punch and Judy wagon shook on its wheels as the horse pawed and stamped impatiently.

"Hi, you there!" cried the rider, beckoning to Mr. Hicks, who was peering from between the curtains in amazement. "Come over here and be quick about it!"

Mr. Hicks hurried to do so. Indeed he did not even stop to hang Mr. Punch back on his hook, but kept him still on one hand. Toby tried hard to hear what the soldier was saying, but he was too far away on his perch and besides, such a lot of people ran out from nearby doorways, and they made such a noise, that he couldn't make out more than a word or two. He saw the rider give Master a bit of paper that seemed to please him greatly. Master nodded his head a great many times and kept pulling at his forelock and grinning in a queer kind of way.

"Remember now," the soldier said as he wheeled his horse about smartly, "half after three and mind you're there on the dot."

"'Alf after three," Mr. Hicks repeated after him, his mouth still gaping open in astonishment. "We'll be there, Toby 'n me."

When the last clatter of the horse's hoofs had died away Mr. Hicks began to recover a little and to say things under his breath that showed how astonished he was. Toby couldn't make them out and he was already completely dazed by what had happened. He knew that it was something extraordinarily fine and in some mysterious way concerned him too. The keeper of the toyshop and the man who sold hot chestnuts both clapped him on the back and all the rest crowded round eagerly.

"Talk about your luck," Toby heard one of them say, "and 'by command.' Well, I never."

"H'it's fair took me off my feet," said Mr. Hicks, though Toby noticed that he still seemed to be standing on them as well as ever. "Can't 'ardly credit my senses. Well, Toby boy, you 'n me 'ave got a sight to do afore this time tomorrow. Time we was gettin' 'ome."

There were plenty of hands to help Mr. Hicks fold up the stage and pack it in the barrow that night, and the toyshop man insisted upon their both coming in to warm themselves a bit before his fire. Toby was so excited at finding himself among the toys he had stared at so long from a distance that he hardly knew how to behave. Indeed he did almost disgrace himself when an ugly Jack-in-the-Box flew out at him, and if it had been within reach he would surely have treated it as he did Mr. Punch's hooked nose. How beautiful the dolls looked so near, even more lovely than from the other side of the window. There was a beautiful little wax figure in pink who danced on her toes on top of one music box and a yellow old mandarin who nodded his head in time to the tune on another. The toyshop man's wife came out from a back room and when she heard that Mr. Hicks and Toby were going to play "by command" next day, she flung up both hands in wonder.

"And to think they was right here in my shop and I didn't know it," her husband kept repeating. "Well, Hicks, I don't begrudge you your luck and just so no one shall say I'm small I'm going to make your Toby there a present of the finest red ribbon bow a dog ever wore around his neck."

They had collected a great many things besides the ribbon by the time they reached home. First Master changed the paper the soldier had given him for a great many shillings and sixpences and even several half crowns. After that he bought a whole bottle of beer, not just a mug as he usually did, and some tobacco and a whole

platter of roast beef and onions and the biggest bone Toby had ever had. Toby was more pleased with this than the cake of soap and the scrubbing brush which was the last purchase. He somehow felt that they were to concern him intimately before the evening was over and he was right.

First it was beef and bones and onions. Then Master called to the landlady to bring him another scuttleful of coal and a kettle of heating water. He also asked for a loan of her wooden washtub, and carried it himself up the five long flights of stairs. Toby had to be dragged from under the bed by his tail. By the time the water was hot enough to make suds, it was well on towards midnight and the Christmas waits were already going about singing in the streets below. Their voices rose shrill and clear on

the frosty air. Toby could hear snatches of their carols between the splashings and sloshings of the soap and water as Mr. Hicks gave him the most thorough washing he had ever had.

"God rest you merry, Gentlemen,
Let nothing you dismay—"
Scrub. Scrub. Scrub.

"Remember Christ, the Savior,
Was born on Christmas Day—"
Scrub. Scrub. Scrub.

Then scrub again. It was soap in the eyes and ears and nose. More rinsing, with water enough to drown him, it seemed, and then more soap again. Toby thought it would be the death of him and he felt very sorry to think that he might never know what would be happening next day that Master made such a to-do about. The washing did finally end and he shook himself till the fire hissed with the drops he spattered. Then Master rubbed and dried him with an old piece of flannel and polished him off by combing with his own comb. Toby thought there would surely be nothing left of him in the end, but there still seemed to be, for Mr. Hicks sat back and surveyed him with great approval.

"Toby," he said solemnly, "you're clean for once't in your life an' may it last you for good an' all!"

Toby agreed with him perfectly.

Master was away all the next morning. He would not take Toby with him for fear he might spoil his fine looks before afternoon. Three o'clock found them out on the streets, Toby riding atop the show wagon as Master pushed it along before him. He had on the new red ribbon and his best ruff and the hole in his plush coat had been neatly darned the night before. Even Master was all smartened up for the holiday in a new muffler, with a big blue glass stickpin in the middle. They did not stop to set the show up, no matter what good corners they came to, but went on and on.

Just as Toby was beginning to wonder if they would ever reach their destination, they came to a high gate with gold lions about it and another soldier in a red coat standing at attention by a queer little house just big enough to hold him if it should happen to rain. Toby felt rather awed as they came alongside and Master pulled a card out of his pocket and handed it over. Another soldier now joined the first one and they both looked at the card and asked Mr. Hicks some questions which Toby was too excited to hear. Next thing he knew they were following the second soldier through the gate and up a driveway towards the most enormous stone house he had ever seen. It seemed to Toby that it must be almost as big as Saint Paul's and the Tower of London put together only it didn't look like either of them.

Master was making a queer hoarse sound in his throat, as if he, too, didn't quite know what to make of all this.

"Keep your 'ead up, Toby boy," he said softly as they

came up to the great carved doors. "Don't you go and let Bucking'am Palace take the stuffin' out o' you!"

Buckingham Palace! Toby's head began to reel so he didn't know what was happening next. In fact he didn't know when or how they got inside. Then they were in an enormous room with so much gold and red velvet Toby scarcely dared look beyond his own nose. Servants in livery were hurrying to and fro, arranging chairs and tables and hanging trinkets on a tall Christmas tree that stood at the far end of the room; others were lighting hundreds of candles in great crystal chandeliers that hung from the ceiling, and Mr. Hicks was setting up the Punch and Judy Show behind a high carved screen. Nobody paid any attention to Toby and so he gathered up courage enough to do a little exploring on his own account.

Here a new surprise awaited him. As he trotted out over the miraculously soft carpet he beheld a dog advancing to meet him. It came nearer and nearer and the queer thing about it was that it, too, wore a ruff and a red ribbon and a plush coat. He turned about uncertainly and there beside it was another exactly like the first. He flew in another direction, nearly colliding with a servant bearing a great tray of cakes, only to catch glimpses of more Toby dogs, and still more, little yellow dogs in ruffs in every direction. He forgot his awe of Buckingham Palace and flew at the nearest one, teeth bared and ears up. His claws slid against something smooth and his nose went bang against a cool something. Then one of the servants laughed and carried him back to Master.

"Tryin' to fight 'imself in the mirrors, the little chap was," he explained, while Toby grinned sheepishly.

Still, it was a relief to find there weren't really all those other Dog Tobys to be his rivals.

Now Master lifted him up to his place on the stage and they waited for the party to begin. Toby knew it was a party, for he had heard the word pass from one footman to another. He felt almost as scared and excited as the time he had first played his part, and it seemed as if the great gold doors would never open. He could peer through a carved place in the screen and see all that was going on. The Christmas tree was a blaze of light now and all the tinsel and colored balls shone like fairy fruits. Now a music box began to play the sweetest tunes and the doors opened wide to let in a company of children—little girls in sashes and curls and stiffly starched dresses and little boys in velvet jackets and round white collars. All the mouths were smiling and all the eyes held little bright glints from the Christmas tree candles and all the feet began to skip and caper.

Then some one was lifting the screen away from the show wagon and Toby suddenly saw that the children were all hurrying after a lady with smoothly parted hair and rustling skirts, and a tall gentleman in whiskers and a soldier's coat with medals and yards and yards of gold braid. Between them were two children and Toby could hardly keep from barking for joy when he saw that one was the Little Boy of yesterday afternoon. There was no mistaking him even if he had not worn his gay

Scotch kilts. His fair hair shone in the candlelight and when he saw what was standing behind the screen he dropped the lady's hand and ran straight up to the show wagon. Toby was so glad to see him again that he stood right up and barked though he knew it wasn't the right time for that, but nobody seemed to mind his doing it at all.

"Here is your surprise, Eddie," said the lady, "the very same Punch and Judy Show that you saw by the arcade yesterday, only you must remember never to run away from Mademoiselle to see one again."

"Yes," said the Little Boy, drawing a long breath, "it's the same Little Dog Toby. Please can't it begin?"

So Toby and the puppets and Mr. Hicks played their parts and all the children pressed as close and squealed and laughed and clapped as hard as those at any street corner or country fair. Toby had never barked or growled or bitten and shaken Mr. Punch so beautifully. He wasn't afraid any longer. He even took pleasure in turning to look at himself in all the long mirrors on the walls. Over and over they acted it and the candles burned out on the tree and the cakes and jellies and tarts waited untasted on the tables. The Little Boy could never have enough and his eyes never left the painted stage.

"Come," said the lady, bending over him, "Dog Toby must be tired now, and the others want to open their presents and have their tea."

The Little Boy would not go till the gentleman in whiskers had lifted him up so that he could pat Dog Toby

himself. It was a proud moment and Mr. Hicks came out and stood grinning nearby. The Little Boy's hand was very clean and soft as he stroked him. Toby suddenly felt very glad that Master had given him that hard scrubbing last night. He put out his pink tongue and gave the plump fingers several licks.

"I wish he were my Little Dog Toby," said the Little Boy.

Mr. Hicks looked rather serious at this, but the tall man only smiled and set the child on his feet.

By the time Master had folded the stage up, all the children were busy eating cakes and drinking their cambric tea.

"Come along, Toby," he said, moving towards the door which two servants were opening for them, "we can go 'ome now."

They went back to High Holborn stuffed full of roast goose and plum pudding from the servants' hall. Master's pockets bulged with oranges and nuts and raisins and gingerbread, and Toby had a royal beef bone to take home. Surely no dog ever had such a Christmas.

Tired as they were after it all, Master sat up late painting a gold crown to go with the moon and stars above the Punch and Judy Stage. He printed red letters on a big placard for Toby to wear round his neck, and this is what they said:

DOG TOBY,
BY SPECIAL APPOINTMENT TO
HIS ROYAL HIGHNESS, PRINCE OF WALES.

The Caravan

RUTH SAWYER

IT WAS WINTER—and twelve months since the gipsies had driven their flocks of mountain sheep over the dark, gloomy Balkans, and had settled in the southlands near to the Aegean. It was twelve months since they had seen a wonderful star appear in the sky and heard the singing of angelic voices afar off.

They had marveled much concerning the star until a runner had passed them from the south bringing them news that the star had marked the birth of a Child whom the wise men had hailed as "King of Israel" and "Prince of Peace." This had made Herod of Judea both afraid and angry and he had sent soldiers secretly to kill the Child; but in the night they had miraculously disappeared —the Child with Mary and Joseph—and no one knew whither they had gone. Therefore Herod had sent runners all over the lands that bordered the Mediterranean with a message forbidding every one giving food or shelter or warmth to the Child, under penalty of death. For Herod's anger was far-reaching and where his anger fell there fell his sword likewise. Having given his warning, the runner passed on, leaving the gipsies to marvel much over the tale they had heard and the meaning of the star.

Now on that day that marked the end of the twelve months since the star had shone the gipsies said among themselves: "Dost thou think that the star will shine again tonight? If it were true, what the runner said, that when it shone twelve months ago it marked the place where the Child lay it may even mark His hiding-place this night. Then Herod would know where to find Him, and send his soldiers again to slay Him. That would be a cruel thing to happen!"

The air was chill with the winter frost, even there in the southland, close to the Aegean; and the gipsies built high their fire and hung their kettle full of millet, fish, and bitter herbs for their supper. The king lay on his couch of tiger-skins, and on his arms were amulets of heavy gold, while rings of gold were on his fingers and in his ears. His tunic was of heavy silk covered with a leopard cloak, and on his feet were shoes of goatskin trimmed with fur. Now, as they feasted around the fire a voice came to them through the darkness, calling. It was a man's voice, climbing the mountains from the south.

"Ohe! Ohe!" he shouted. And then nearer, "O-he!"

The gipsies were still disputing among themselves whence the voice came when there walked in the circle about the fire a tall, shaggy man, grizzled with age, and a sweet-faced young mother carrying a child.

"We are outcasts," said the man, hoarsely. "Ye must know that whosoever succors us will bring Herod's vengeance like a sword about his head. For a year we have wandered homeless and cursed over the world. Only the wild creatures have not feared to share their food and give us shelter in their lairs. But tonight we can go no farther; and we beg the warmth of your fire and food enough to stay us until the morrow."

The king looked at them long before he made reply. He saw the weariness in their eyes and the famine in their cheeks; he saw, as well, the holy light that hung about the child, and he said at last to his men:

"It is the Child of Bethlehem, the one they call the 'Prince of Peace.' As yon man says, who shelters them shelters the wrath of Herod as well. Shall we let them tarry?"

One of their numbers sprang to his feet, crying: "It is a sin to turn strangers from the fire, a greater sin if they be poor and friendless. And what is a king's wrath to us? I say bid them welcome. What say the rest?"

And with one accord the gipsies shouted, "Yea, let them tarry!"

They brought fresh skins and threw them down beside the fire for the man and woman to rest on. They brought them food and wine, and goat's milk for the Child; and when they had seen all was made comfortable for them they gathered round the Child—these black gipsy men—to touch His small white hands and feel His golden hair. They brought Him a chain of gold to play with and another for His neck and tiny arm.

"See, these shall be Thy gifts, little One," said they, "the gifts for Thy first birthday."

And long after all had fallen asleep the Child lay on His bed of skins beside the blazing fire and watched the light dance on the beads of gold. He laughed and clapped His hands together to see the pretty sight they made; and then a bird called out of the thicket close by.

"Little Child of Bethlehem," it called, "I, too, have a birth gift for Thee. I will sing Thy cradle song this night." And softly, like the tinkling of a silver bell and like clear water running over mossy places, the nightingale sang and sang, filling the air with melodies.

And then another voice called to him:

"Little Child of Bethlehem, I am only a tree with boughs all bare, for the winter has stolen my green cloak, but I also can give Thee a birth gift. I can give Thee shelter from the biting north wind that blows." And the tree bent low its branches and twined a rooftree and a wall about the Child.

Soon the Child was fast asleep, and while He slept a small brown bird hopped out of the thicket. Cocking his little head, he said:

"What can I be giving the Child of Bethlehem? I could fetch Him a fat worm to eat or catch Him the beetle that crawls on yonder bush, but He would not like that! And I could tell Him a story of the lands of the north, but

45

He is asleep and would not hear." And the brown bird shook its head quite sorrowfully. Then it saw that the wind was bringing the sparks from the fire nearer and nearer to the sleeping Child.

"I know what I can do," said the bird, joyously. "I can catch the hot sparks on my breast, for if one should fall upon the Child it would burn Him grievously."

So the small brown bird spread wide his wings and caught the sparks on his own brown breast. So many fell that the feathers were burned; and burned was the flesh beneath until the breast was no longer brown, but red.

Next morning, when the gipsies awoke, they found Mary and Joseph and the Child gone. For Herod had died, and an angel had come in the night and carried them back to the land of Judea. But the good God blessed those who had cared that night for the Child.

To the nightingale He said: "Your song shall be the sweetest in all the world, for ever and ever; and only you shall sing the long night through."

To the tree He said: "Little fir-tree, never more shall your branches be bare. Winter and summer you and your seedlings shall stay green, ever green."

Last of all He blessed the brown bird: "Faithful little watcher, from this night forth you and your children shall have red breasts, that the world may never forget your gift to the Child of Bethlehem."

The Gift of the Magi

O. HENRY

ONE DOLLAR and eighty-seven cents. That was all. And sixty cents of it was in pennies. Pennies saved one and two at a time by bulldozing the grocer and the vegetable man and the butcher until one's cheeks burned with the silent imputation of parsimony that such close dealing implied. Three times Della counted it. One dollar and eighty-seven cents. And the next day would be Christmas.

There was clearly nothing to do but flop down on the shabby little couch and howl. So Della did it. Which instigates the moral reflection that life is made up of sobs, sniffles, and smiles, with sniffles predominating.

While the mistress of the home is gradually subsiding from the first stage to the second, take a look at the home. A furnished flat at eight dollars per week. It did not exactly beggar description, but it certainly had that word on the lookout for the mendicancy squad.

In the vestibule below was a letter-box into which

no letter would go, and an electric button from which no mortal finger could coax a ring. Also appertaining thereunto was a card bearing the name "Mr. James Dillingham Young."

The "Dillingham" had been flung to the breeze during a former period of prosperity when its possessor was being paid thirty dollars per week. Now, when the income was shrunk to twenty dollars, the letters of "Dillingham" looked blurred, as though they were thinking seriously of contracting to a modest and unassuming D. But whenever Mr. James Dillingham Young came home and reached his flat above he was called "Jim" and greatly hugged by Mrs. James Dillingham Young, already introduced to you as Della. Which is all very good.

Della finished her cry and attended to her cheeks with a powder puff. She stood by the window and looked out dully at a gray cat walking a gray fence in a gray back yard. Tomorrow would be Christmas Day, and she had only $1.87 with which to buy Jim a present. She had been saving every penny she could for months, with this result. Twenty dollars a week doesn't go far. Expenses had been greater than she had calculated. They always are. Only $1.87 to buy a present for Jim. Her Jim. Many a happy hour she had spent planning for something nice for him. Something fine and rare and sterling—something just a little bit near to being worthy of the honor of being owned by Jim.

There was a pier glass between the windows of the

room. Perhaps you have seen a pier glass in an eight-dollar flat. A very thin and very agile person may, by observing his reflection in a rapid sequence of longitudinal strips, obtain a fairly accurate conception of his looks. Della, being slender, had mastered the art.

Suddenly she whirled from the window and stood before the glass. Her eyes were shining brilliantly, but her face had lost its color within twenty seconds. Rapidly she pulled down her hair and let it fall to its full length.

Now, there were two possessions of the James Dillingham Youngs in which they both took a mighty pride. One was Jim's gold watch that had been his father's and his grandfather's. The other was Della's hair. Had the Queen of Sheba lived in the flat across the airshaft, Della would have let her hair hang out the window some day to dry just to depreciate Her Majesty's jewels and gifts. Had King Solomon been the janitor, with all his treasures piled up in the basement, Jim would have pulled out his watch every time he passed, just to see him pluck at his beard from envy.

So now Della's beautiful hair fell about her, rippling and shining like a cascade of brown waters. She did it up again nervously and quickly. Once she faltered for a minute while a tear splashed on the worn red carpet.

On went her old brown jacket; on went her old brown hat. With a whirl of skirts and with the brilliant sparkle still in her eyes, she fluttered out the door and down the stairs to the street.

Where she stopped the sign read: "Mme. Sofronie. Hair Goods of All Kinds." One flight up Della ran, and collected herself, panting. Madame, large, too white, chilly, hardly looked the "Sofronie."

"Will you buy my hair?" asked Della.

"I buy hair," said Madame. "Take yer hat off and let's have a sight at the looks of it."

Down rippled the brown cascade.

"Twenty dollars," said Madame, lifting the mass with a practiced hand.

"Give it to me quick," said Della.

Oh, and the next two hours tripped on rosy wings. Forget the hashed metaphor. She was ransacking the stores for Jim's present.

She found it at last. It surely had been made for Jim and no one else. There was no other like it in any of the stores, and she had turned all of them inside out. It was a platinum watch-chain, simple and chaste in design, properly proclaiming its value by substance alone and not by meretricious ornamentation—as all good things should do. It was even worthy of The Watch. As soon as she saw it she knew that it must be Jim's. It was like him. Quietness and value—the description applied to both. Twenty-one dollars they took from her for it, and she hurried home with the eighty-seven cents. With that chain on his watch Jim might be properly anxious about the time in any company. Grand as the watch was, he sometimes looked at it on the sly on account of the shabby old leather strap that he used in place of a proper gold chain.

When Della reached home her intoxication gave way a little to prudence and reason. She got out her curling-irons and lighted the gas and went to work repairing the ravages made by generosity added to love. Which is always a tremendous task, dear friends—a mammoth task.

Within forty minutes her head was covered with tiny close-lying curls that made her look wonderfully like a truant schoolboy. She looked at her reflection in the mirror long, carefully, and critically.

"If Jim doesn't kill me," she said to herself, "before he takes a second look at me, he'll say I look like a Coney Island chorus girl. But what could I do—oh! what could I do with a dollar and eighty-seven cents?"

At seven o'clock the coffee was made and the frying-pan was on the back of the stove, hot and ready to cook the chops.

Jim was never late, Della doubled the watch chain in her hand and sat on the corner of the table near the door that he always entered. Then she heard his step on the stair away down on the first flight, and she turned white for just a moment. She had a habit of saying little silent prayers about the simplest everyday things, and now she whispered: "Please, God, make him think I am still pretty."

The door opened and Jim stepped in and closed it. He looked thin and very serious. Poor fellow, he was only twenty-two—and to be burdened with a family! He needed a new overcoat and he was without gloves.

Jim stepped inside the door, as immovable as a setter at the scent of quail. His eyes were fixed upon Della, and there was an expression in them that she could not read, and it terrified her. It was not anger, nor surprise, nor disapproval, nor horror, nor any of the sentiments that she had been prepared for. He simply stared at her fixedly with that peculiar expression on his face.

Della wriggled off the table and went for him.

"Jim, darling," she cried, "don't look at me that way. I had my hair cut off and sold it because I couldn't have lived through Christmas without giving you a present. It'll grow out again—you won't mind, will you? I just had to do it. My hair grows awfully fast. Say 'Merry Christmas!' Jim, and let's be happy. You don't know what a nice—what a beautiful, nice gift I've got for you."

"You've cut off your hair?" asked Jim, laboriously, as if he had not arrived at that patent fact yet even after the hardest mental labor.

"Cut it off and sold it," said Della. "Don't you like me just as well, anyhow? I'm me without my hair, ain't I?"

Jim looked about the room curiously.

"You say your hair is gone?" he said, with an air almost of idiocy.

"You needn't look for it," said Della. "It's sold, I tell you—sold and gone, too. It's Christmas Eve, boy. Be good to me, for it went for you. Maybe the hairs of my head were numbered," she went on with a sudden serious sweetness, "but nobody could ever count my love for you. Shall I put the chops on, Jim?"

Out of his trance Jim seemed to quickly wake. He enfolded his Della. For ten seconds let us regard with discreet scrutiny some inconsequential object in the other direction. Eight dollars a week or a million a year—what is the difference? A mathematician or a wit would give you the wrong answer. The Magi brought valuable gifts, but that was not among them. This dark assertion will be illuminated later on.

Jim drew a package from his overcoat pocket and threw it upon the table.

"Don't make any mistake, Dell," he said, "about me. I don't think there's anything in the way of a haircut or a shave or a shampoo that could make me like my girl any less. But if you'll unwrap that package you may see why you had me going awhile at first."

White fingers and nimble tore at the string and paper. And then an ecstatic scream of joy; and then, alas! a quick feminine change to hysterical tears and wails, necessitating the immediate employment of all the comforting powers of the lord of the flat.

For there lay The Combs—the set of combs that Della had worshiped for long in a Broadway window. Beautiful combs, pure tortoise shell, with jeweled rims—just the shade to wear in the beautiful vanished hair. They were expensive combs, she knew, and her heart had simply craved and yearned over them without the least hope of possession. And now they were hers, but the tresses that should have adorned the coveted adornments were gone.

But she hugged them to her bosom, and at length she was able to look up with dim eyes and a smile and say: "My hair grows so fast, Jim!"

And then Della leaped up like a little singed cat and cried, "Oh, oh!"

Jim had not yet seen his beautiful present. She held it out to him eagerly upon her open palm. The dull precious metal seemed to flash with a reflection of her bright and ardent spirit.

"Isn't it a dandy, Jim? I hunted all over town to find it. You'll have to look at the time a hundred times a day now. Give me your watch. I want to see how it looks on it."

Instead of obeying, Jim tumbled down on the couch and put his hands under the back of his head and smiled.

"Dell," said he, "let's put our Christmas presents away and keep 'em awhile. They're too nice to use just at present. I sold the watch to get the money to buy your combs. And now suppose you put the chops on."

The Magi, as you know, were wise men—wonderfully wise men—who brought gifts to the Babe in the manger. They invented the art of giving Christmas presents. Being wise, their gifts were no doubt wise ones, possibly bearing the privilege of exchange in case of duplication. And here I have lamely related to you the uneventful chronicle of two foolish children in a flat who most unwisely sacrificed for each other the greatest treasures of their house. But in a last word to the wise of these days let it be said that of all who give gifts these two were the wisest. Of all who give and receive gifts, such as they are the wisest. Everywhere they are the wisest. They are the Magi.

The Holy Night

SELMA LAGERLÖF

IT WAS a Christmas Day and all the folks had driven to church except grandmother and me. I believe we were all alone in the house. We had not been permitted to go along, because one of us was too old and the other was too young. And we were sad, both of us, because we had not been taken to early mass to hear the singing and to see the Christmas candles.

But as we sat there in our loneliness, grandmother began to tell a story.

"There was a man," said she, "who went out in the dark night to borrow live coals to kindle a fire. He went from hut to hut and knocked. 'Dear Friends, help me!'

said he. 'My wife has just given birth to a child, and I must make a fire to warm her and the little one.'

"But it was 'way in the night, and all the people were asleep. No one replied.

"The man walked and walked. At last he saw the gleam of a fire a long way off. Then he went in that direction, and saw that the fire was burning in the open. A lot of sheep were sleeping around the fire, and an old shepherd sat and watched over the flock.

"When the man who wanted to borrow fire came up to the sheep, he saw that three big dogs lay asleep at the shepherd's feet. All three awoke when the man approached and opened their great jaws, as though they wanted to bark; but not a sound was heard. The man noticed that the hair on their backs stood up and that their sharp, white teeth glistened in the firelight. They dashed toward him. He felt that one of them bit at his leg and one at his hand and that one clung to his throat. But their jaws and teeth wouldn't obey them, and the man didn't suffer the least harm.

"Now the man wished to go farther, to get what he needed. But the sheep lay back to back and so close to one another that he couldn't pass them. Then the man stepped upon their backs and walked over them and up to the fire. And not one of the animals awoke or moved."

Thus far, grandmother had been allowed to narrate without interruption. But at this point I couldn't help breaking in. "Why didn't they do it, grandma?" I asked.

"That you shall hear in a moment," said grandmother—and went on with her story.

"When the man had almost reached the fire, the shepherd looked up. He was a surly old man, who was unfriendly and harsh toward human beings. And when he saw the strange man coming, he seized the long spiked staff, which he always held in his hand when he tended his flock, and threw it at him. The staff came right toward the man, but, before it reached him, it turned off to one side and whizzed past him, far out in the meadow."

When grandmother had got this far, I interrupted her again. "Grandma, why wouldn't the stick hurt the man?" Grandmother did not bother about answering me, but continued her story.

"Now the man came up to the shepherd and said to him: 'Good man, help me, and lend me a little fire! My wife has just given birth to a child, and I must make a fire to warm her and the little one.'

"The shepherd would rather have said no, but when he pondered that the dogs couldn't hurt the man, and the sheep had not run from him, and that the staff had not wished to strike him, he was a little afraid, and dared not deny the man that which he asked.

" 'Take as much as you need!' he said to the man.

"But then the fire was nearly burnt out. There were no logs or branches left, only a big heap of live coals; and the stranger had neither spade nor shovel, wherein he could carry the red-hot coals.

"When the shepherd saw this, he said again: 'Take as much as you need!' And he was glad that the man wouldn't be able to take away any coals.

"But the man stooped and picked coals from the ashes with his bare hands, and laid them in his mantle. And he didn't burn his hands when he touched them, nor did the coals scorch his mantle; but he carried them away as if they had been nuts or apples."

But here the story-teller was interrupted for the third time. "Grandma, why wouldn't the coals burn the man?"

"That you shall hear," said grandmother, and went on:

"And when the shepherd, who was such a cruel and hard-hearted man, saw all this, he began to wonder to himself: 'What kind of a night is this, when the dogs do not bite, the sheep are not scared, the staff does not kill, or the fire scorch?' He called the stranger back, and said to him: 'What kind of a night is this? And how does it happen that all things show you compassion?'

"Then said the man: 'I cannot tell you if you yourself do not see it.' And he wished to go his way, that he might soon make a fire and warm his wife and child.

"But the shepherd did not wish to lose sight of the man before he had found out what all this might portend. He got up and followed the man till they came to the place where he lived.

"Then the shepherd saw that the man didn't have so much as a hut to dwell in, but that his wife and babe were lying in a mountain grotto, where there was nothing except the cold and naked stone walls.

"But the shepherd thought that perhaps the poor innocent child might freeze to death there in the grotto; and, although he was a hard man, he was touched, and thought he would like to help it. And he loosened his knapsack from his shoulder, took from it a soft white sheepskin,

winged angels, and each held a stringed instrument, and all sang in loud tones that to-night the Saviour was born who should redeem the world from its sins.

"Then he understood how all things were so happy this night that they didn't want to do anything wrong.

"And it was not only around the shepherd that there were angels, but he saw them everywhere. They sat inside the grotto, they sat outside on the mountain, and they flew under the heavens. They came marching in great companies, and, as they passed, they paused and cast a glance at the child.

"There were such jubilation and such gladness and songs and play! And all this he saw in the dark night, whereas before he could not have made out anything. He was so happy because his eyes had been opened that he fell upon his knees and thanked God."

Here grandmother sighed and said: "What that shepherd saw we might also see, for the angels fly down from heaven every Christmas Eve, if we could only see them."

Then grandmother laid her hand on my head, and said: "You must remember this, for it is as true, as true as that I see you and you see me. It is not revealed by the light of lamps or candles, and it does not depend upon sun and moon; but that which is needful is, that we have such eyes as can see God's glory."

gave it to the strange man, and said that he should let the child sleep on it.

"But just as soon as he showed that he, too, could be merciful, his eyes were opened, and he saw what he had not been able to see before and heard what he could not have heard before.

"He saw that all around him stood a ring of little silver-

A Child's Christmas in Wales

An Excerpt from the book by

DYLAN THOMAS

"OUR SNOW was not only shaken from whitewash buckets down the sky, it came shawling out of the ground and swam and drifted out of the arms and hands and bodies of the trees; snow grew overnight on the roofs of the houses like a pure and grandfather moss, minutely white-ivied the walls and settled on the postman, opening the gate, like a dumb, numb thunderstorm of white, torn Christmas cards."

"Were there postmen then, too?"

"With spring eyes and wind-cherried noses, on spread, frozen feet they crunched up to the doors and mittened on them manfully. But all that the children could hear was a ringing of bells."

"You mean that the postman went rat-a-tat-tat and the doors rang?"

"I mean that the bells that the children could hear were inside them."

"I only hear thunder sometimes, never bells."

"There were church bells, too."

"Inside them?"

"No, no, no, in the bat-black, snow-white belfries, tugged by bishops and storks. And they rang their tidings over the bandaged town, over the frozen foam of the powder and ice-cream hills, over the crackling sea. It seemed that all the churches boomed for joy under my window; and the weathercocks crew for Christmas, on our fence."

Our Brother is Born

HARRY AND ELEANOR FARJEON

Now every child that dwells on earth,
Stand up, stand up and sing:
The passing night has given birth
Unto the children's king.
Sing sweet as the flute,
Sing clear as the horn,
Sing joy for the children,
Come Christmas morn:

*Little Christ Jesus
Our brother is born.*

To His Saviour, A Child,
A Present By A Child

ROBERT HERRICK

Go pretty child, and bear this flower
Unto thy little Saviour;
And tell Him, by that bud now blown,
He is the Rose of Sharon known;
When thou hast said so, stick it there
Upon His bib, or stomacher:
And tell Him (for good handsell too)
That thou hast brought a whistle new,
Made of a clean straight oaken reed,
To charm His cries (at time of need;)
Tell Him, for coral, thou hast none;
But if thou hadst, He should have one;
But poor thou art, and knows to be
Even as moneyless as He.
Lastly, if thou canst win a kiss
From those mellifluous lips of His;
Then never take a second on,
To spoil the first impression.

'Twas the Night Before Christmas

(A Visit from St. Nicholas)

CLEMENT C. MOORE

'Twas the night before Christmas, when all through the house
Not a creature was stirring, not even a mouse;

The stockings were hung by the chimney with care,
In hopes that St. Nicholas soon would be there;
The children were nestled all snug in their beds,
While visions of sugar-plums danced through their heads;
While mamma in her kerchief, and I in my cap,
Had just settled our brains for a long winter's nap,—
When out on the lawn there arose such a clatter,
I sprang from my bed to see what was the matter.

Away to the window I flew like a flash,
Tore open the shutters and threw up the sash.
The moon, on the breast of the new-fallen snow,
Gave a luster of midday to objects below;
When what to my wondering eyes should appear,
But a miniature sleigh and eight tiny reindeer,
With a little old driver, so lively and quick
I knew in a moment it must be St. Nick.
More rapid than eagles his coursers they came,
And he whistled and shouted and called them by name.

"Now, Dasher! now, Dancer! now, Prancer and Vixen!
On, Comet! on, Cupid! on, Donder and Blitzen!
To the top of the porch, to the top of the wall!
Now, dash away, dash away, dash away all!"

As dry leaves that before the wild hurricane fly,
When they meet with an obstacle, mount to the sky,
So, up to the house-top the coursers they flew,
With a sleigh full of toys,—and St. Nicholas, too.

58

And then in a twinkling I heard on the roof
The prancing and pawing of each little hoof,
As I drew in my head and was turning around,
Down the chimney St. Nicholas came with a bound.

He was dressed all in fur from his head to his foot,
And his clothes were all tarnished with ashes and soot;
A bundle of toys he had flung on his back,
And he looked like a peddler just opening his pack.
His eyes how they twinkled! his dimples how merry!
His cheeks were like roses, his nose like a cherry;
His droll little mouth was drawn up like a bow,
And the beard on his chin was as white as the snow.

The stump of a pipe he held tight in his teeth,
And the smoke of it encircled his head like a wreath.
He had a broad face, and a little round belly
That shook, when he laughed, like a bowl full of jelly.
He was chubby and plump,—a right jolly old elf—
And I laughed when I saw him, in spite of myself.
A wink of his eye and a twist of his head
Soon gave me to know I had nothing to dread.

He spoke not a word, but went straight to his work,
And filled all the stockings; then turned with a jerk,
And laying his finger aside of his nose,
And giving a nod, up the chimney he rose.
He sprang to his sleigh, to his team gave a whistle,
And away they all flew like the down of a thistle;

But I heard him exclaim, ere he drove out of sight:
"Happy Christmas to all, and to all a good night!"

An Alphabet of Christmas

ANONYMOUS

A   for the Animals out in the stable.
B   for the Babe in their manger for cradle.

C   for the Carols so blithe and gay.
D   for December, the twenty-fifth day.

E   for the Eve when we're all so excited.
F   for the Fire when the Yule Log is lighted.
G   is the Goose which you all know is fat.

H   is the Holly you stick in your hat.
I   for the Ivy which clings to the wall.

J   is for Jesus the cause of it all.
K   for the Kindness begot by this feast.
L   is the Light shining way in the East.

M   for the Mistletoe. Beware where it hangs!

N   is the Nowell the angels first sang.

O   for the Oxen, the first to adore Him.
P   for the Presents wise men laid before Him.
Q   for the Queerness that this should have been,
     near two thousand years before you were seen.

R   for the Romps and the Raisins and Nuts.
S   for the Stockings that Santa Claus stuffs.

T   for the Toys on the Christmas Tree hanging.
U   is for Us over all the world ranging.
V   for the Visitors welcomed so warmly.
W   for the Waits at your door singing heartily!

XYZ   bother me! all I can say,
       Is this is the end of my Christmas lay.
       So now to you all, wherever you may be,
       A merry merry Christmas, and may many you see!

Feeding Birds

RUMER GODDEN

"Scatter us crumbs, we
midget are your charity."

Charity starts in a nest,
the human breast;
like birds
it needs no words
but sings
when it is given;
has wings
to lift
the spirit up,
by gift
of this small water cup,
to heaven;
and warm and light as feathers the bread
spared to see creation fed.

Love in a crumb is a mystery;
bread is the Body of charity;
little nerves of finch or tit
fly down to feast and quicken it;
robin, blackbird, sparrow, wren,
feasted, quicken it in men."

As Dew in Aprille

ANONYMOUS

I sing of a maiden
That is makeles:
King of all kings
To her son she ches.

He came al so stille
There his moder was,
As dew in Aprille
That falleth on the grass.

He came al so stille
To his moder's bour,
As dew in Aprille
That falleth on the flour.

He came al so stille
There his moder lay,
As dew in Aprille
That falleth on the spray.

Moder and maiden
Was never none but she:
Well may such a lady
Goddes moder be.

63

A Christmas Carol

GILBERT K. CHESTERTON

The Christ-child lay on Mary's lap,
His hair was like a light.
(O weary, weary were the world,
But here is all aright.)

The Christ-child lay on Mary's breast,
His hair was like a star,
(O stern and cunning are the kings,
But here the true hearts are.)

The Christ-child lay on Mary's heart,
His hair was like a fire.
(O weary, weary is the world,
But here the world's desire.)

The Christ-child stood at Mary's knee,
His hair was like a crown,
And all the flowers looked up at Him,
And all the stars looked down.

Christmas Carol

KENNETH GRAHAME

Villagers all, this frosty tide,
Let your doors swing open wide,
Though wind may follow and snow betide
Yet draw us in by your fire to bide:
Joy shall be yours in the morning.

Here we stand in the cold and the sleet,
Blowing fingers and stamping feet,
Come from far away, you to greet—
You by the fire and we in the street—
Bidding you joy in the morning.

For ere one half of the night was gone,
Sudden a star has led us on,
Raining bliss and benison—
Bliss tomorrow and more anon,
Joy for every morning.

Good man Joseph toiled through the snow—
Saw the star o'er the stable low;
Mary she might not further go—

Welcome thatch and litter below!
Joy was hers in the morning.

And then they heard the angels tell,
"Who were the first to cry Nowell?
Animals all as it befel,
In the stable where they did dwell!
Joy shall be theirs in the morning."

The Twelve Days of Christmas

OLD ENGLISH OR SCOTTISH AIR

ARR. BY JAMES MOREHEAD

66

On the first day of Christ - mas My

true love sent to me, A par - tridge in a pear tree. On the

sec - ond day of Christ - mas My true love sent to me,

Two tur - tle doves, and a par - tridge in a pear

tree. On the third day of Christ-mas My true love sent to me,

Three French hens, two tur-tle doves, and a

par - tridge in a pear tree. On the

4.

fourth day of Christ - mas My true love sent to me,

67

68

four call - ing birds, three French hens,

two tur - tle doves, and a par - tridge in a pear tree. On the

REPEAT THROUGH NO. 12, ADDING ONE LINE EACH REPETITION.

Sixth day of Christ - mas My true love sent to me

Seventh day etc. . . . .

59

6. Six geese a - lay - ing,
7. Seven swans a - swim - ming,
8. Eight maids a - milk - ing,
9. Nine la - dies danc - ing,   five gold rings,
10. Ten lords a - leap - ing,
11. Eleven pi - pers pip - ing,
12. Twelve drum - mers drum - ming,

four call - ing birds, three French hens, two tur - tle doves, and a

Through 11th day repeat. | *Final ending after 12th day.*

par - tridge in a pear tree.   On the tree.

The Holly and the Ivy

TRADITIONAL

OLD FRENCH MELODY, 1861

The hol - ly and the i - vy, Now both are full well grown, — Of

all the trees that are in the wood, The hol - ly bears the crown. —

O the ris - ing of the sun, The run-ning of the deer, — The play-ing of the

or - gan, Sweet sing-ing in the choir, — Sweet sing - ing in the choir. —

Bring a Torch, Jeanette, Isabella

TRANS. BY E. CUTHBERT NUNN

OLD FRENCH AIR, POSSIBLY 17TH CENT.

ARR. BY NICK NICHOLSON

72

2. It is wrong when the Child is sleeping,
   It is wrong to talk so loud.
   Silence, all, as you gather around,
   Lest your noise should waken Jesus:
   Hush! Hush! see how fast He slumbers;
   Hush! Hush! see how fast He sleeps!

3. Softly to the little stable,
   Softly for a moment come!
   Look and see how charming is Jesus,
   How He is white, His cheeks are rosy!
   Hush! Hush! see how the Child is sleeping;
   Hush! Hush! see how He smiles in dreams!

We Wish You a Merry Christmas

TRADITIONAL

OLD ENGLISH OR SCOTTISH AIR

ARR. BY NICK NICHOLSON

74

2. Now bring us some figgy pudding,
   Now bring us some figgy pudding,
   Now bring us some figgy pudding,
   And bring it out here.
   REFRAIN

3. We won't go until we get some,
   We won't go until we get some,
   We won't go until we get some,
   So bring some out here.
   REFRAIN

4. We all love figgy pudding,
   We all love figgy pudding,
   We all love figgy pudding,
   So bring some out here.
   REFRAIN

5. We wish you a Merry Christmas,
   We wish you a Merry Christmas,
   We wish you a Merry Christmas
   And a Happy New Year!
   REFRAIN

75

The Cherry Tree Carol

TRADITIONAL

OLD ENGLISH AIR

1. — Jo - seph was an old man, An— old man was
2. — As they went a - walk - ing In the gar - den so

he: He mar - ried sweet Ma — ry, The— Queen of Ga - li - lee.
gay, Maid Ma - ry spied cher - ries, Hang-ing o - ver yon— tree.

76

3. Mary said to Joseph
With her sweet lips so mild,
"Pluck those cherries, Joseph,
For to give to my Child."

4. "O then," replied Joseph
With words so unkind,
"I will pluck no cherries
For to give to thy Child."

5. Mary said to cherry tree,
"Bow down to my knee,
That I may pluck cherries
By one, two, and three."

6. The uppermost sprig then
Bowed down to her knee:
"Thus you may see, Joseph,
These cherries are for me."

7. "O eat your cherries, Mary,
   O eat your cherries now,
   O eat your cherries, Mary,
   That grow upon the bough."

8. As Joseph was a-walking
   He heard Angels sing,
   This night there shall be born
   Our heavenly King.

9. "He neither shall be born
   In house nor in hall,
   Nor in the place of Paradise,
   But in an ox-stall.

10. "He shall not be clothed
    in Purple nor pall;
    But all in fair linen,
    As wear babies all.

11. "He shall not be rocked,
    In silver nor gold,
    But in a wooden cradle
    That rocks on the mould.

12. "He neither shall be christened
    In milk nor in wine,
    But in pure spring-well water
    Fresh sprung from Bethine."

13. Mary took her Baby,
    She dressed Him so sweet,
    She laid Him in a manger
    All there for to sleep.

14. As she stood over Him
    She heard Angels sing,
    "Oh! bless our dear Savior,
    Our heavenly King."

78

2. Led by the light
   Of faith serenely beaming,
   With glowing hearts by His cradle we stand;
   So led by light of
   A star sweetly gleaming,
   Here came the Wise Men from Orient land.
   The King of kings lay thus in lowly manger,
   In all our trials born to be our friend;
   He knows our need,
   To our weakness is no stranger!
   Behold your king,
   Before Him lowly bend!
   Behold your King,
   Before Him lowly bend!

3. Truly He taught us
   To love one another;
   His law is love,
   And His gospel is peace;
   Chains shall he break
   For the slave is our brother,
   And in His name all oppression shall cease.
   Sweet hymns of joy in grateful chorus raise we,
   Let all within us praise His holy name;
   Christ is the Lord,
   Oh, praise His name forever!
   His pow'r and glory
   Ever more proclaim!
   His pow'r and glory
   Ever more proclaim!

O Holy Night!

ADOLPHE ADAM

79

world _____ in sin and er - ror pin - - ing, Till He ap-

peared and the soul felt its worth. A thrill of hope the

wea - ry soul re-joic - es, For yon-der breaks a new and glo-rious morn; _____

Fall   on your knees,   Oh, hear ___ the an-gel voi - ces! O

night ___ di - vine, ___ O night ___ when Christ was born! O

night, ___ O ho - ly night O night di - vine!

night,   O ho - ly ___ night,   O night di - vine!

Here We Come A-Caroling

TRADITIONAL

OLD ENGLISH WASSAIL SONG

ARR. BY TORSTEIN O. KVAMME

82

Here we come a car-ol-ing A-mong the leaves so green; —

Here we come a - wan - d'ring, So fair___ to be seen.

REFRAIN

Love and joy come to you, And to you glad Christ-mas too; And God bless you and

send___you a hap-py New Year, And God send you a hap-py New___ Year.

2. We are not daily beggars
   That beg from door to door;
   But we are neighbors' children,
   Whom you have seen before.
                    REFRAIN

Good master and good mistress,
As you sit by the fire,
Pray think of us poor children,
Who wander in the mire.
                    REFRAIN

God bless the master of this house,
Likewise the mistress, too,
And all the little children,
That round the table go.
                    REFRAIN

It Came Upon the Midnight Clear

EDMUND H. SEARS, 1850   RICHARD S. WILLIS, 1851

It came up-on the mid-night clear, That glo-rious song of old,—

From an-gels bend-ing near the earth, To touch their harps of gold:—

"Peace on the earth, good will to men From heav'n's all gra-cious King,"—

The world in sol-emn still-ness lay To hear the an-gels sing.—

84

2. Still thro' the cloven skies they come,
   With peaceful wings unfurled;
   And still their heav'nly music floats
   O'er all the weary world:
   Above its sad and lowly plains
   They bend on hov'ring wing,
   And ever o'er its Babel sounds
   The blessed angels sing.

3. O ye beneath life's crushing load,
   Whose forms are bending low,
   Who toil along the climbing way
   With painful steps and slow;
   Look now, for glad and golden hours
   Come swiftly on the wing;
   O rest beside the weary road
   And hear the angels sing.

4. For lo! the days are hast'ning on,
   By prophets seen of old,
   When with the evercircling years
   Shall come the time foretold,
   When the new heav'n and earth shall own
   The Prince of Peace their King,
   And the whole world send back the song
   Which now the angels sing.

Lo, How a Rose E'er Blooming

TRANS. BY THEODORE BAKER

15TH CENTURY GERMAN

ARR. BY MICHAEL PRAETORIOUS, 1609

Lo, how a Rose e'er bloom- ing From ten- der stem hath sprung! Of Jes-se's lin-eage com-ing As men ___ of old have sung. It came, a flow'r-et bright, ___ A- mid the cold of ___ win- ter, When half ___ spent ___ was the night.

2. Isaiah 'twas foretold it,
   The Rose I have in mind,
   With Mary we behold it,
   The Virgin Mother kind.
   To show God's love aright
   She bore to men a Savior,
   When half spent was the night.

Hark! the Herald Angels Sing

CHARLES WESLEY, 1739

FELIX MENDELSSOHN, 1840
ARR. BY W. H. CUMMINGS, 1855

88

Hark! the her - ald an - gels sing, "Glo - ry to the new-born King! Peace on earth, and

mer - cy mild, — God and sin - ners re-con - ciled." Joy - ful, all ye na - tions, rise, —

Join the tri - umph of the skies; With th'an - gel - ic host pro - claim, "Christ is born in

Beth - le - hem." Hark! the her - ald an - gels sing, "Glo - ry to the new-born King!"

2. Christ, by highest heav'n adored;
   Christ, the everlasting Lord;
   Late in time behold Him come,
   Offspring of the favored one.
   Veiled in flesh, the Godhead see;
   Hail th'incarnate Deity
   Pleased, as man with men to dwell,
   Jesus, our Immanuel!
   Hark! the herald angels sing,
   "Glory to the new-born King!"

3. Hail! the heav'n-born Prince of Peace!
   Hail! the Son of Righteousness!
   Light and life to all He brings,
   Ris'n with healing in His wings.
   Mild He lays His glory by,
   Born that man no more may die:
   Born to raise the sons of earth,
   Born to give them second birth.
   Hark! the herald angels sing,
   "Glory to the new-born King!"

Silent Night

JOSEPH MÖHR, 1818

FRANZ GRÜBER, 1818

90

Si - lent night! Ho - ly night! All is calm, all is bright.

'Round yon vir - gin moth - er and child! Ho - ly In - fant, so ten - der and mild,

Sleep in heav - en - ly peace,____ Sleep in heav - en - ly peace.

2. Silent night! Holy night!
   Shepherds quake at the sight!
   Glories stream from heaven afar,
   Heav'nly hosts sing, "Alleluia!"
   Christ, the Savior, is born!
   Christ, the Savior, is born!

3. Silent night! Holy night!
   Son of God, love's pure light!
   Radiant beams from Thy holy face
   With the dawn of redeeming grace,
   Jesus, Lord at Thy birth,
   Jesus, Lord at Thy birth.

I Saw Three Ships

TRADITIONAL

ARR. BY SIR JOHN STAINER

Allegro

I saw three ships come sail - ing in, On

Christ - mas Day, on Christ - mas Day; I saw three ships come

sail - ing in, On Christ - mas Day in the morn - ing.

93

2. And what was in those ships all three,
On Christmas Day, on Christmas Day;
And what was in those ships all three,
On Christmas Day in the morning.

3. The Virgin Mary and Christ were there,
On Christmas Day, on Christmas Day;
The Virgin Mary and Christ were there,
On Christmas Day in the morning.

Carol of the Birds

94

Whence comes this rush of wings a - far,

Fol - low - ing straight the No - el _ star?

Birds from the woods in won - drous flight,

Beth - le - hem seek this _ Ho - ly _ Night

95

2. "Tell us, ye birds, why come ye here,
   Into this stable, poor and drear?"
   "Hast'ning we seek the new-born King,
   And all our sweetest music bring."

3. Hark! how the greenfinch bears his part,
   Philomel, too, with tender heart,
   Chants from her leafy dark retreat,
   Re, mi, fa, sol, in accents sweet.

4. Angels and shepherds, birds of the sky,
   Come where the Son of God doth lie;
   Christ on earth with man doth dwell,
   Join in the shout, "Noel, Noel!"

The Boar's Head Carol

TRADITIONAL

MODERATO

WYNKYN DE WORDE, 1521

ARR. BY NICK NICHOLSON

96

The boar's head in hand bear I, Be - decked with bays and

rose - ma - ry. And I pray you, my mas - ters be mer - ry Quot

est - is in con - viv - i - o.

Ca - put a - pri de - fe - ro Red - dens lau - des Dom - i - no.

RALL _ _ _ _ _ _ _ _ _ _ _ _

2. The boar's head, I understand,
   The finest dish in all the land.
   Which is thus all bedecked with gay garland,
   Let us *servire cantico*.

   CHORUS

3. The boar's head that we bring here
   Betokeneth a Prince without peer
   Is born this day to buy us dear.
   Noel! Noel! Noel! Noel!

   CHORUS

4. A boar is a sovereign beast
   And acceptable in every feast;
   So might this Lord be to most and least.
   Noel! Noel! Noel! Noel!

   CHORUS

5. This boar's head we bring with song
   In worship of Him that thus sprang
   Of a Virgin to redress all wrong.
   Noel! Noel! Noel! Noel!

   CHORUS

buy=redeem

Deck the Halls

TRADITIONAL

OLD WELSH AIR

98

Deck the hall with boughs of hol - ly, Fa la la la la, la la la la.

'Tis the sea - son to be jol - ly, Fa la la la la, la la la la.

Don we now our gay ap - par - el, Fa la la la la la la,

Troll the an - cient Yule - tide car - ol, Fa, la, la, la, la, la, la, la, la.

2. See the blazing Yule before us,
   Fa la la la la, la la la la.
   Strike the harp and join the chorus,
   Fa la la la la, la la la la.
   Follow me in merry measure,
   Fa la la la la la la la,
   While I tell of Yuletide treasure,
   Fa, la, la, la, la, la, la, la, la.

3. Fast away the old year passes,
   Fa la la la la, la la la la.
   Hail the new, ye lads and lasses,
   Fa la la la la, la la la la.
   Sing we joyous all together,
   Fa la la la la la la la,
   Heedless of the wind and weather,
   Fa, la, la, la, la, la, la, la, la.

Joy to the World!

ISAAC WATTS, 1719

GEORGE F. HANDEL, 1742
ARR. BY LOWELL MASON, 1830

Joy to the world! the Lord is come; Let earth re-

ceive her King;____ Let ev - 'ry heart____ pre-

pare Him room,____ And heav'n and na - ture sing, And

heav'n and na - ture sing, And heav'n, and heav'n___ and na - ture sing.

100

2. Joy to the world! the Savior reigns;
   Let men their songs employ;
   While fields and floods, rocks, hills and plains,
   Repeat the sounding joy,
   Repeat the sounding joy,
   Repeat, repeat the sounding joy.

3. No more let sin and sorrow grow,
   Nor thorns infest the ground;
   He comes to make His blessings flow
   Far as the curse is found,
   Far as the curse is found,
   Far as, far as the curse is found.

4. He rules the world with truth and grace,
   And makes the nations prove
   The glories of His righteousness,
   And wonders of His love,
   And wonders of His love,
   And wonders, and wonders of His love.

The First Noel

TRADITIONAL

16TH CENTURY, FRENCH

102

2. They looked up and saw a star
   Shining in the east beyond them far,
   And to the earth it gave great light.
   And so it continued both day and night.
   CHORUS

3. And by the light of that same star,
   Three wise men came from country far,
   To seek for a King was their intent.
   And to follow the star wherever it went.
   CHORUS

4. This star drew nigh to the northwest,
   O'er Bethlehem it took its rest,
   And there it did both stop and stay
   Right o'er the place where Jesus lay.
   CHORUS

5. Then enter'd in those wise men three,
   Full reverently upon their knee,
   And offer'd there in His presence,
   Their gold and myrrh and frankincense.
   CHORUS

While Shepherds Watched

NAHUM TATE, 1700

ESTE, 1592

While shep - herds watched their flocks by night, All seat - ed on the ground,

The an - gel of the Lord came down, And glo - ry shone a - round.

4. "The heav'nly Babe you there shall find,
   To human view displayed,
   All meanly wrapp'd in swathing bands
   And in a manger laid."

5. Thus spake the seraph and forthwith
   Appear'd a shining throng
   Of angels, praising God, who thus
   Address'd their joyful song:

6. "All glory be to God on high,
   And to the earth be peace;
   Good will henceforth from heav'n to men
   Begin and never cease."

2. "Fear not," said he for mighty dread
   Had seized their troubled minds
   "Glad tidings of great joy I bring,
   To you and all mankind.

3. "To you in David's town this day,
   Is born of David's line
   The Savior, who is Christ the Lord,
   And this shall be the sign.

O Little Town of Bethlehem

PHILLIPS BROOKS, 1868

LEWIS H. REDNER, 1868

O lit - tle town of Beth - le - hem, How still we see thee lie;

A - bove thy deep and dream - less sleep The si - lent stars go by:

Yet in thy dark streets shin - eth The ev - er - last - ing Light;

The hopes and fears of all the years Are met in thee to - night.

2. For Christ is born of Mary;
   And gathered all above,
   While mortals sleep, the angels keep
   Their watch of wond'ring love.
   O morning stars, together
   Proclaim the holy birth;
   And praises sing to God, the King,
   And peace to men on earth.

3. How silently, how silently,
   The wondrous gift is giv'n!
   So God imparts to human hearts
   The blessings of His heav'n.
   No ear may hear His coming,
   But in this world of sin,
   Where meek souls will receive Him, still
   The dear Christ enters in.

4. O holy child of Bethlehem,
   Descend to us, we pray;
   Cast out our sin, and enter in,
   Be born in us today.
   We hear the Christmas angels
   The great glad tidings tell;
   O come to us, abide with us,
   Our Lord Emmanuel.

Noel Sing We

TRADITIONAL

15TH CENTURY ENGLAND

108

2. *De fructu ventris* of Mary bright;
   Both God and man in her alight;
   Out of disease He did us dight,
   Both all and some.
   > BURDEN

3. *Puer natus* to us was sent,
   To bliss us bought, fro bale us blent,
   And else to woe we had y-went,
   Both all and some.
   > BURDEN

4. *Lux fulgebit* with love and light,
   In Mary mild His pennon pight,
   In her took kind with manly might,
   Both all and some.
   > BURDEN

5. *Gloria tibi*, ay and bliss:
   God unto His grace He us wiss,
   The rent of heaven that we not miss,
   Both all and some.
   > BURDEN

Rex pacificus—The Peace-bringing King (Zech. 9:9)
Exortum est—It is risen (Isa. 60:1)
liss—joy
giss—prepare
De fructu ventris—Of the fruit of the womb (Luke 1:42)
disease—misery
dight—put
Puer natus—A boy (new-) born (Isa. 9:6)
bale—evil, destruction
blent—turned away
And else—or else
y'-went—gone
Lux fulgebit—The light will shine (Isa. 9:2)
pight—pitched
kind—nature
Gloria tibi—Glory be to Thee
wiss—guide
rent—reward

Away in a Manger

15TH CENTURY GERMAN
ARR. BY NICK NICHOLSON

1. A-way in a man-ger no crib for a bed, The
2. The cat-tle are low-ing, the poor ba-by wakes, But

lit-tle Lord Je-sus laid down His sweet head, The
lit-tle Lord Je-sus, no cry-ing He makes, I

stars in the sky,------looked down where He lay, The
love Thee, Lord Je-sus, look down ·from the sky, And

lit-tle Lord Je-sus, a-sleep on the hay.
stay by my cra-dle, till morn-ing is nigh.

2. Sing, choirs of Angels, sing in exultation,
   Sing all ye citizens of heav'n above:
   Glory to God in the highest, glory!
   O come, let us adore Him,
   O come, let us adore Him,
   O come, let us adore Him,
   Christ the Lord.

1. *Adeste fideles, laeti triumphantes;*
   Venite, venite in Bethlehem;
   Natum videte, Regem angelorum:
   Venite adoremus,
   Venite adoremus,
   Venite adoremus
   Dominum.

2. *Cantet nunc Io! Chorus angelorum;*
   Cantet nunc aula coelestium:
   Gloria, gloria in excelsis Deo!
   Venite adoremus,
   Venite adoremus,
   Venite adoremus,
   Dominum.

O Come, All Ye Faithful

17TH CENTURY LATIN

TRANS. BY F. OAKELEY, 1852

WADE, 1751

O come, all ye faith - ful, Joy - ful and tri - umph - ant, O
come ye, O come ye to Beth - le - hem. Come and be -
hold Him, Born the King of An - gels: O come, let us a - dore Him, O
come, let us a - dore Him, O come, let us a - dore Him, Christ the Lord.

Jingle Bells

J. S. PIERPONT, 1857

Dash-ing thro' the snow   in a   one horse o - pen sleigh;

O'er the fields we go,   laugh-ing all the way;   Bells on bob-tail ring,

mak-ing spir - its bright; What fun it is to ride and sing a sleigh-ing song to-night!

Refrain

Jin-gle bells, jin-gle bells, jin-gle all   the way!   Oh, what fun it is to ride in a

114

one-horse o-pen sleigh! — Jin-gle bells, jin-gle bells, jin-gle all the way!

Oh, what fun it is to ride in a one-horse o-pen sleigh!

2. A day or two ago
   I thought I'd take a ride,
   And soon Miss Fannie Bright
   Was seated by my side.
   The horse was lean and lank;
   Misfortune seemed his lot;
   He got into a drifted bank
   And we, we got up-sot.
                    REFRAIN

3. Now the ground is white;
   Go it while you're young;
   Take the girls tonight,
   And sing this sleighing song.
   Just get a bobtailed bay,
   Two-forty as his speed;
   Hitch him to an open sleigh,
   And crack, you'll take the lead.
                    REFRAIN

The Coventry Carol

ROBERT CROO, 1534

ENGLISH MELODY, 1591
ARR. BY NICK NICHOLSON

2. O sisters, too, how may we do,
   For to preserve this day;
   This poor Youngling for whom we sing,
   Bye, bye, lully, lullay.

3. Herod the King, in his raging,
   Charged he hath this day;
   His men of might, in his own sight,
   All children young to slay.

4. Then woe is me, poor Child, for thee,
   And ever mourn and say;
   For thy parting nor say nor sing,
   Bye, bye, lully, lullay.

117

Angels From the Realms of Glory

JAMES MONTGOMERY, 1816

HENRY SMART, 1867

118

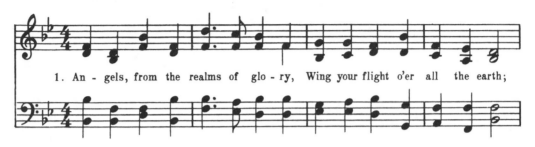

1. An - gels, from the realms of glo - ry, Wing your flight o'er all the earth;

Ye who sang cre - a - tion's sto - ry, Now pro - claim Mes - si - ah's birth:

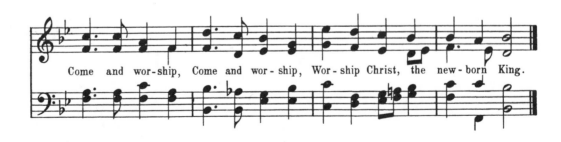

Come and wor - ship, Come and wor - ship, Wor - ship Christ, the new - born King.

2. Shepherds, in the field abiding,
   Watching o'er your flocks by night,
   God with man is now residing,
   Yonder shines the infant light;
   Come and worship, come and worship,
   Worship Christ, the new-born King.

3. Sages, leave your contemplations,
   Brighter visions beam afar;
   Seek the great Desire of nations,
   Ye have seen His natal star:
   Come and worship, come and worship,
   Worship Christ, the new-born King.

4. Saints before the altar bending,
   Watching long in hope and fear,
   Suddenly the Lord, descending,
   In His temple, shall appear:
   Come and worship, come and worship,
   Worship Christ, the new-born King.

Angels We Have Heard on High

TRADITIONAL

OLD FRENCH MELODY

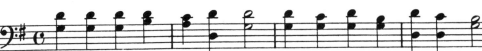

An - gels we have heard on high, Sweet - ly sing - ing o'er the plains;

And the moun - tains in re - ply Ech - o - ing their joy - ous strains.

2. Shepherds, why this jubilee?
Why your joyous songs prolong?
What the gladsome tidings be
Which inspire your heavenly song?

REFRAIN

3. Come to Bethlehem, and see
Him whose birth the angels sing;
Come adore on bended knee,
Christ, the Lord, our new-born King.

REFRAIN

2. Why lies He in such mean estate,
   Where ox and ass are feeding?
   Good Christian, fear: for sinner here
   The silent Word is pleading:
                    REFRAIN

3. So bring Him incense, gold, and myrrh,
   Come peasant, king to own Him;
   The King of kings salvation brings;
   Let loving hearts enthrone Him.
                    REFRAIN

What Child is This?

WILLIAM C. DIX

OLD ENGLISH AIR, "GREENSLEEVES"
ARR. BY SIR JOHN STAINER

What Child is this, Who, laid to rest On Ma- ry's lap is

sleep - ing? Whom an-gels greet with an-thems sweet, While shep-herds watch are keep-ing?

This, this is Christ the King; Whom shep-herds guard and an - gels sing:

Haste, haste to bring Him laud, The Babe, the Son of Ma- ry!

We Three Kings of Orient Are

JOHN H. HOPKINS, JR., 1857

JOHN H. HOPKINS, JR.

We three kings of O - ri - ent are, Bear - ing gifts we trav - erse
far Field and foun - tain, moor and moun - tain, Fol - low - ing yon - der Star.
Oh, star of won - der, star of might, Star with roy - al beau - ty bright,
West - ward lead - ing, still pro - ceed - ing, Guide us to the per - fect light.

2. Born a babe on Bethlehem's plain,
   Gold we bring to crown Him again;
   King forever, ceasing never,
   Over us all to reign.
   REFRAIN

3. Frankincense to offer have I;
   Incense owns a Deity nigh,
   Pray'r and praising all men raising,
   Worship God on high.
   REFRAIN

4. Myrrh is mine; its bitter perfume
   Breathes a life of gath'ring gloom;
   Sorrowing, sighing, bleeding, dying,
   Sealed in the stone-cold tomb.
   REFRAIN

5. Glorious now behold Him rise,
   King and God and Sacrifice;
   Heav'n sings "Hallelujah!"
   "Hallelujah!" earth replies.
   REFRAIN

THE LEGEND OF THE RAVEN

The raven was the herald of Christ's birth. According to the legend, the raven was flying one night over the fields of Bethlehem when suddenly the sky was filled with angels. They told him the good tidings and the raven flew off at once to tell the joyous news to the other birds. The little wren lovingly wove a small blanket of feathers and green leaves and moss to keep the Baby warm; and for this she is known as *la poulette de Dieu* in France. At daybreak the cock announced the event to the world. He was very formal, so he spoke in Latin. "*Christus natus est!*" he proclaimed from the rooftops. The nightingale sang the Baby a lullaby, and the robin shielded Him from the fierce heat of the open fire. But on that long-ago Christmas night it was the wise raven who first heard the angels tell of the Holy Child Who was born in the stable.

THE OX'S CAKE

Because the humble farm animals gave the infant Jesus his first shelter, and warmed him with their breath, it is said that they were rewarded by the gift of human speech on Christmas Eve. In most countries, however, it is considered very bad luck to overhear them conversing, so no one has ever reported doing so.

Animals are very much a part of Christmas celebrations in all countries, especially in farming villages. Extra food is given them, and sometimes there is even ale for the horses.

In earlier days in Herefordshire, England, the wassailers carried the festive bowl into the cow barn, where toasts were drunk to all the farm animals. A big round cake with a hole in the center was placed on the horn of an ox, who, of course, promptly tossed it off. If it landed behind him it brought good luck for the new year to the farmer's wife; if it landed in front the luck was claimed by the estate steward.

In some parts of Poland, before the Christmas Eve dinner, some unleavened bread is given to all members of the family and to the horses and cows. Then the family sits down to a feast at a table on which wheat and straw have been spread in memory of Jesus's birth in a stable.

St. Francis of Assisi, who loved all animals, said they should be included in Christmas celebrations "for reverence of the Son of God Whom on such a night the most Blessed Virgin did lay down in a stall between the ox and the ass."

THE ROSEMARY LEGEND

It is said that when the Holy Family fled to Egypt, they stopped to rest on a hillside, by a little stream where Mary washed the baby's clothes. She spread his tiny garments on a fragrant bush to dry in the sun. For its humble service the plant was named rosemary, and God rewarded it with delicate blossoms of the same heavenly blue as the Madonna's robe.

Rosemary that has decorated the altar at Christmastime brings special blessings to the recipient, and protection against evil spirits, according to medieval legend.

THE BIRD TREE

At Christmas time, especially in very cold places like Scandinavia, birds are given special treats. In Sweden they have what they call the bird tree. This is a wheel that is raised on a tall pole in the farmyard. On the wheel are placed sheaves of corn or wheat for the birds. Handfuls of grain are also placed on windowsills, roofs, and garden walls.

In rural Poland a sheaf of wheat stands in a corner of every room of the house on Christmas Eve. These are later taken out to the orchard, both as charms to ensure a plentiful harvest and as a feast for the birds.

THE LEGEND OF THE LUCIA QUEEN

In Sweden there is a particularly charming Christmas custom centering about the Lucia Queen. Saint Lucia was a beautiful Christian maiden who lived many centuries ago in Rome. Because she refused to give up her religion to marry a pagan, she was burned at the stake by order of the Emperor Diocletian. Her saint's day falls on December 13th, a day that was celebrated even in pre-Christian Sweden as the beginning of the Festival of Light—the Winter Solstice, the day when they say that "the sun stands still." Because Saint Lucia's festival coincided with the time of year when daylight once more began to lengthen she was especially beloved by these people living where winter nights were very long and dark.

In Swedish homes today, the youngest daughter is usually chosen to be the Lucia Queen. On Christmas morning, wearing a white gown and a crown of lighted candles, she brings breakfast and a Christmas song to all the members of her household. The animals are never forgotten; they, too, receive extra rations so they may share in the joy and good will of the day.

In some places a Lucia Queen is elected for an entire village, to reign over all the holiday festivities. On Christ-

mas day, in the early morning darkness, she sets out with a tray of food and coffee to bring her message of the coming revival of the light, as well as of peace and prosperity to all the homes and farms. The animals also receive special holiday foods from the Lucia Queen.

In her train a colorful procession follows: a man on horseback, "star boys" and maids of honor bearing candles, and many other young people dressed as Biblical characters or as the mythical demons and trolls who have been conquered by the returning sunlight.

132

THE LEGEND OF THE HOLY THORN

In England the Holy Thorn still blooms at midnight on January 5th, the date of the Old Christmas Eve. The calendar was changed in 1752 and the Christmas festival was moved backward to its present date, but the tree remains faithful to the earlier calendar.

The Holy Thorn comes from the thornwood staff of St. Joseph of Arimathea. Long ago, it is said, when he was in Britain preaching, he visited Glastonbury, where he thrust his staff into the ground as he rested. There it rooted itself and grew, and every year since then it has blossomed on January 5th.

Cuttings of the original Glastonbury Thorn (which was destroyed by the Puritans, who did not approve of Christmas celebrations) were fortunately taken and planted elsewhere, and some of these are still alive today. There is one in the ruins of Glastonbury Abbey and another in Herefordshire. More than once it has been recorded that these winter-flowering hawthorns have bloomed precisely at midnight of Old Christmas Eve.

THE BLOSSOMING TREE

A German legend says that from time to time, over the centuries, simple and good folk have seen, on Christmas Eve, a single tree in the dark winter forest in full bloom, glowing with light, and with a beautiful child sitting in its branches. A pope, asked to comment on this radiant vision explained that "the blossoming tree is humanity; the shining lights are good men; and the Child is the Savior." Today, the fir tree, resplendent with candles or electric lights, shining decorations, paper flowers and candy fruits has become a nearly universal, traditional reminder of the miraculous blossoming of trees on Christmas Eve.

134

THE KISSING BOUGH

Mistletoe, the Golden Bough of legend, has come to be a part of our Christmas celebrations, but its roots are deep in pre-Christian custom. The ancient Scandinavians held it in awe as its powerful spirit was supposed to have killed the sun-god, Baldur the Beautiful. But they also called it Allheal, as it was used to cure many ills and was revered as the plant of peace, beneath which enemies were reconciled.

Perhaps it was this last use which led to the custom of kissing under the mistletoe. This pleasant tradition has persisted down through centuries, especially in England. There the kissing bough was, until Victorian times, a center of holiday festivities during the twelve days of Christmas.

A double hoop or wreath of greens, decorated with paper roses, red apples, sweets, and candles, would be hung in the center of the hall, just above the heads of the tallest guests. From its center hung the mistletoe and any girl who stood beneath it could be kissed by anyone present. Gifts were sometimes suspended from the bough on long ribbons.

TWELFTH NIGHT

The end of the twelve days of Christmas is the Epiphany, when the wise men arrived in Bethlehem to pay homage to the Holy Child. Until the last century, nearly every German, French, or English family had an elaborate Twelfth Night Cake, decorated with figures of the three kings. This was the time for putting away the Christmas decorations, too, for the next day work would be resumed.

But many of the old customs connected with Twelfth Night seem to have been handed down from pre-Christian times. The Scottish *Up Helly-aa* ceremony at the climax of which a replica of a Viking ship is set afire seems to be connected with ancient Scandinavian winter solstice festivals, celebrating the return of daylight to the winter-dark world.

Other customs seem to come from old farm festivals which have been combined with Christian symbolism. Thus, in parts of rural England groups of men still go out on Old Twelfth Night with lanterns and guns, which they shoot off among the tree-branches to frighten away bad spirits and to bring good luck and plenty. Cider is poured around the roots of the fruit trees and cider-soaked

cakes are placed in the branches. A song is sung to the trees, asking them to bear plenty of fruit:

"... Hats full, caps full,
Threescore baskets full,
And all our pockets full, too."

CHRISTMAS AT TUDORS' FARM

Christmas is the most joyous season of the year for Tasha Tudor and her family, and their celebration of this holiday embraces both the reverently religious and the festive secular aspects, in the New England tradition. The Tudors live in a rambling seventeen-room farmhouse in the heart of the New Hampshire hills. The red frame house, built in 1789, was bought by the Tudors from the grandson of the original builder, so it has had only two families living in it. On the rolling land is a large stand of timber, providing not only the family Christmas trees, but lumber for the barns and wood for the wide, old-fashioned fireplaces.

Preparations for the next Christmas begin almost as soon as the ornaments from the one before are put away, for many of the gifts, certainly the most meaningful ones, are made lovingly by hand and take a long time to complete. Tasha Tudor says, "Christmas is one of our most exciting celebrations and we spend months planning a marionette show and making presents for this special time of year. In the long, back room of the house known as the winter kitchen, there is a large fireplace and brick oven, such as may be found in most old New England houses. Here stands the settle and behind it is the Christmas chest. Into this chest, the year 'round, go presents and surprises of all shapes and sizes. Certain drawers and closets, too, are forbidden territory."

THE ADVENT CALENDARS

By October it is time for Tasha to start to draw her yearly Advent calendar. Each year, taking turns, one of the children chooses the subject for the calendar, which Tasha Tudor will make. Perhaps it will be a cozy village of field mice: numbered doors and windows open, one for each day of Advent, to reveal the mice at their winter activities. One may be sleeping, with a tiny red-and-white stocking cap on his head; another reading a book; another trimming a Christmas tree; still another rocking a baby mouse in a little wooden cradle. Another year the calendar may be about the pre-Christmas doings in Corgiville, a village inhabited, of course, by Welsh corgi dogs. The new calendar occupies a place of honor on the wall of the living room, but all the calendars from previous years are also hung up on the first day of Advent.

ST. NICHOLAS' BIRTHDAY

St. Nicholas' birthday, December 6th, is the real beginning of the Christmas season for the Tudors, as it is for many families not only in this country but also in Holland, France and England. Tasha says, "A lot happens on this special day at tea time. The morning has been spent in setting up the crèche and decorating the winter kitchen. The old Noah's Ark and its inmates are set up on the long mantle. The Advent wreath is hung and it is time for tea. Now the Christmas cake is cut and the prettiest cookies are brought out. How beautiful it all looks—the curtained stage for the marionette show at one end of the room, the logs burning peacefully in the great fireplace, the fragrant greens, the lovely shadows of the Advent wreath and its ribbons on the ceiling, the crèche with its candles lighting the nativity scene.

KRISS KRINGLE

"After tea we sing carols around the melodeon and then, before we go to bed, the old Canton china soup tureen is brought out and from it each member of the family draws a name for his Kriss Kringle. Kriss Kringle is fun. You draw a name and then every day, and in secret, you have to do some nice thing for the person whose name you have. On Christmas Eve itself you guess, or try to guess, who your Kriss Kringle was."

CHRISTMAS CAKE

The Christmas cake has to be made several weeks ahead of time, and kept in a cool place to ripen to its full deliciousness.

2 cups of real butter, scant
1½ cup granulated sugar
8 eggs
1 cup blanched chopped almonds
1 cup chopped citron
5 cups cake flour, not sifted before measuring
1 teaspoon salt
2 teaspoons baking powder
2 cups raisins
3 cups currants
4 tablespoons orange juice
2 teaspoons vanilla
1 cup candied cherries, whole ones

Cream butter, add sugar, mixing well as you do so. Then add eggs, one at a time, beating 5 minutes with hand eggbeater after adding each egg. Add orange juice, vanilla, and almonds.

Sift flour and salt and baking powder into a large bowl. Now add fruit and mix with your hands until fruit is well floured. Then add to first mixture and stir well.

Put in broad pans lined with aluminum foil. Decorate tops with more candied cherries and almonds. Bake about an hour in 275° oven. Makes several cakes, according to size pans used. Wrap in foil and keep in a cool place.

and father. The wreath is hung on December 6th, and the four candles are lighted when the family gathers for tea and Christmas cake. From that day on, a part of each afternoon will be devoted to preparations for Christmas: making presents, planning the marionette show, making the puppets and their costumes, planning and making special gifts for the doll family, and making candies, cakes and cookies. The Christmas chest is filling up, and in the big, cool, storage pantry children sample some of the holiday goodies.

CHRISTMAS SUGAR COOKIES

- 1 pound of (*real*) butter
- 2 eggs
- 5 cups all-purpose flour
- 2 cups sugar
- a pinch of salt
- 1 tablespoon vanilla
- 1 teaspoon baking soda dissolved in
- 3 tablespoons milk

Put all ingredients in a bowl and mix with hands until a smooth dough is formed. No amount of mixing seems to bother it. Form into a ball, dust with flour and chill thoroughly before using.

Then break into conveniently sized pieces, probably adding a bit more flour to each bit of dough to make it easier to handle, and roll out.

Roll as thin as possible, dust with granulated sugar and

THE ADVENT WREATH

The rich red ribbons on the Advent wreath have a story of their own. They were originally used to tie back the church pews at the wedding of Tasha Tudor's mother

nutmeg and cut into shapes. Bake until light brown in 350° oven (about twelve minutes). The recipe makes five or six dozen cookies.

Ground almonds or nuts of any sort may be added to all or part of dough. The Tudors always add ground almonds to one batch which they then cut with a flower-shaped cutter and place half a candied cherry on each. They are very pretty. The others are decorated with chocolate bits, melted and forced through a paper cornucopia.

Cookies can be made far in advance and wrapped in foil or kept in tin boxes in a cool place.

MAKING AND FILLING CORNUCOPIAS

At Christmas time children of friends and neighbors know that each of them will find on the Tudors' tree a cornucopia filled with candy, a "clear toy," a Christmas cookie, and a gingerbread toy made just for him. Making the cornucopias of colored paper and filling them with homemade candies is done by the Tudor children, who also make strings of popcorn and cranberries to decorate the tree.

The "clear toys" are not made by the Tudors, but are ordered from one of the few places (Keithen's, in Sunbury, Pennsylvania) still making this candy treat from your grandmother's day. Made of pure barley sugar in brilliant clear colors, they sparkle like bits of stained glass, formed into charming little bugles and drums, elephants and lions, ballet dancers and flowers. The arrival of the "clear toys" is always one of the high spots of the pre-Christmas days.

The Tudor children make the other candies, however, and even the boys have some favorite recipes (which, like many New Englanders, they call "receipts").

TOM'S MAPLE FUDGE

1 7/8 cup XXXX sugar

1 cup maple syrup—*real* maple syrup

½ cup heavy cream

1 cup nuts, chopped, if you want nuts; it's good without

Boil maple syrup, sugar, and cream in heavy saucepan to soft ball stage (234°). Set aside until lukewarm. Beat like fudge until thick, add nuts and pour into buttered pan. Makes about one pound. Cut when cool and wrap each piece individually in aluminum foil.

SETH'S FUDGE

3 squares cooking chocolate

2 cups sugar

¼ teaspoon salt

⅔ cup milk

2 tablespoons light corn syrup

2 tablespoons butter

1 teaspoon vanilla

Chop up squares of chocolate and put in heavy saucepan with sugar, salt, milk and syrup. Place over LOW heat, stir until mixture boils. This takes a while, about twenty minutes, so have a book to read while stirring. Then cook to stage where it will form a soft ball in water (234° on a candy thermometer). Remove from heat, stir in butter and cool to lukewarm. Add vanilla and stir vigorously about 5 minutes and turn into a large bread tin, buttered. Makes about a pound. Cut when cool and wrap each piece like Tom's Maple Fudge.

CHRISTMAS BUTTER TOFFEE

1 cup sugar

½ teaspoon salt

¼ cup water

½ cup butter

½ cup chopped cashew nuts

2 6-ounce packages semi-sweet chocolate bits

Mix together and cook to light crack (285° on a candy thermometer, or until brittle when dropped in water). Add ½ cup of chopped cashew nuts. Pour onto greased cookie sheet. Cool.

Melt 2 6-ounce packages of semisweet chocolate bits. Spread half on top of cooled toffee. Sprinkle with ½ cup of chopped nuts. Cool, turn and repeat the same on the other side. Break in pieces and wrap like fudge. Makes about one pound.

BRINGING IN THE TREE

Christmas Eve is filled with excitement. The Tudors rise early and do the farm chores so the rest of the day can be given over to seasonal delights. Later in the day they will have the dolls' Christmas. But first and foremost is getting the Christmas tree. Finding the right one takes some time but finally from their large planting of fir trees a perfect one is selected, cut down, and brought home on the sled all cold, and smelling deliciously of Christmas. Megan, one of the Welsh corgi dogs, does her bit by bringing in a sprig of greens.

HANGING STOCKINGS

Gathered around the melodeon, the children have sung the beautiful old traditional carols. The farm animals have been fed and bedded down in the warm stable across the yard which, with its rough-timbered ceiling and its loft filled with sweet-smelling hay, cannot be much different from the one that sheltered the holy Baby in Bethlehem long ago. Although it is not yet trimmed, the Christmas tree has been set up in the winter kitchen, and the house is filled with the fragrance of pine. Now is the time for hanging stockings over the broad, old-fashioned fireplace. Some cookies are left for St. Nicholas, too, who will surely be hungry after he has filled the stockings. And some carrots and apples are set out for his hard-working reindeer. Caleb, the corgi, is left to be Santa's reception committee.

THE ANIMALS' CHRISTMAS

Ever since the first Christmas, when the farm animals gave warmth and shelter to the newborn Prince of Peace and His family, the friendly beasts have been especially blessed and remembered at Christmas time.

Cows, pigs, sheep, ducks, gray geese, chickens, horses—both great Belgian workhorses for pulling the plow and shaggy ponies for riding—cats with kittens, a large and amiable bloodhound who thinks she is a lapdog, a canary, and a family of Welsh corgies are all beloved members of

the Tudor farmstead. The animals frequently serve as models for Tasha Tudor, and some, like Dorcus Porcus the pig and Alexander the gander have been the subjects of books.

Special holiday treats are given to all the animals on Christmas morning: hot mash for the hens and geese, apples and carrots for the cows and horses. For each dog a delectable bone is hung with the children's stockings, and each cat gets a catnip mouse.

THE BIRDS' CHRISTMAS

Birds, too, must be remembered at Christmas time, for these gentle creatures were much loved by the Christ child. For the wild birds the Tudors make balls of peanut butter, raisins and chopped nuts. These are then chilled in the refrigerator until hard. On Christmas day, they are tied to tree branches. Such fare would be too rich, however, for the pet canary, who gets a chicory salad in a little flower pot.

When Tasha Tudor was a child, her mother (the portrait painter, Rosamond Tudor) kept several hives of honey bees. At Christmas time the hives were decorated with holly sprigs, and Tasha Tudor has continued this custom.

MAKING MARIONETTES

The Tudors' marionette show has grown from a simple family entertainment to a production of real artistry. The entire show is planned and produced by the family. "Making the marionettes is fun," says Tasha Tudor, "though a bit on the untidy side as far as housekeeping goes. Clay, plaster casts, wood, the contents of a scrap bag, nails, glue, sewing baskets are all assembled in the winter kitchen and the real kitchen, even spreading to the best parlor at tea time. The dogs love it for there is always something interesting to chew. We try to get the show well under way by November so we can rehearse three times a week until Christmas."

A stage, which fits perfectly a section of the living room, is easily put up or taken down for storage. The marionettes are large string puppets (about 18″ tall) made by Tasha Tudor and the children each year. The heads are usually modeled first in clay and then cast in plaster-of-paris molds. Sometimes the heads are made of papier maché, or of plastic wood, which can be carved and sanded and then painted realistically. Hands and feet are made of wood, and the bodies of wood, cloth or wire. Sometimes the characters in the plays are animals, as for instance, in *The Brementown Musicians*. The cock for this play was made of wire and muslin which was covered with real chicken feathers donated by the barnyard cock. Yellow cloth wrapped over wires formed legs and claws, and bright red flannel made his comb and wattles.

THE MARIONETTE SHOW

The plays are taken from favorite stories: folk and fairy tales, stories of King Arthur's knights, myths and legends. Parts are largely ad-libbed, as all are thoroughly familiar with the story. They do rehearse a great deal, however, so as to be sure that all will go well, but the informality and spontaneity of the performance is part of the fun.

As Tasha Tudor describes it, "A few days after Christmas we give the Christmas party and marionette show. At four on the day selected, guests of all ages arrive. We always hope it won't snow too much for we live well out in the country. All the cookies and cakes and little tarts are now brought out and set on platters. The silver tea set has been polished and every available cup and saucer is spread out on the table. Furniture is moved out of the winter kitchen to make room for chairs and benches for grownups. If you are under fifteen you sit on the floor. There is a general excitement, especially amongst the puppeteers back-stage, hoping that all will go well. It always seems to, but still it is a great relief when the play is successfully done.

"Then tea is served—a huge delectable tea—with grandmothers and grandfathers and aunts and uncles and cousins and friends all fitting in somehow and admiring the gingerbread castle which has now been lighted. Before the guests go home the big tree, too, is lighted and each child collects his loot—a gingerbread animal, a 'clear toy,' and a full cornucopia."

THE GINGERBREAD CASTLE

"We always make a special cookie for each member of the family and for the children of friends and neighbors. Besides the shaped cookies, we also make an elaborate gingerbread castle. The size and shape of the house or castle is decided upon and sketched. Then it is cut out of cardboard and the cut pieces of cardboard are used as templates or guides in shaping the gingerbread dough on the baking sheet, before cooking. Holes are pierced along the sides of the gingerbread slabs. When they are baked, the slabs fit together quite nicely, rather like a prefabricated house. They are laced together firmly with ordinary white string. Traces of the holes made before baking remain as indentations in the cooked slabs, making it easier to thread the string through them. When the castle is frosted, the lacings do not show."

CHRISTMAS TREE GINGERBREAD

1 cup shortening
1 cup light brown sugar
3 eggs, well beaten
1½ cups molasses
6 cups bread flour
1½ tablespoons ground ginger
2¼ teaspoons salt
1½ teaspoons baking soda
1 teaspoon cinnamon

Cream shortening and add sugar, eggs, and molasses.
Sift dry ingredients and add them to the first mixture.
Chill and roll out, not too thinly. Cut into shapes to hang on the tree or make into walls for a gingerbread castle. Bake on flat sheets in 350° oven until dry but not crisp, about fifteen minutes. This recipe will make one small castle, or many shaped cookies. Decorate with the following frosting, forced through a paper cornucopia.

FROSTING

1½ cups sugar
½ cup water
2 *fresh* egg whites

Boil sugar and water together until they spin a fine hair when blown upon. Now get someone to help you pour the hot syrup over the two egg whites which you have already beaten (by hand, with an egg-beater) dry and stiff. You beat again while the other person pours the syrup on in a fine stream, turning the bowl as he does it. The frosting should now be nice and thick, ready for use.

THE DOLLS' CHRISTMAS

Over the years, the Tudors' doll family has taken on a life of its own, and the dolls' Christmas celebration on December 24th has become a family tradition. So lifelike and enchanting is the world of the dolls that friends of the Tudors have also become fascinated by it, and often the dolls receive gifts or cards from faraway friends in the real world. But let Tasha Tudor describe the doll family's Christmas in her own words:

"We also have a doll family who celebrate along with us and they have presents, too. They are not ordinary dolls at all. They live in the Hotel Black Walnut in the upstairs spare room. There are four dolls: Captain and Mrs. Thaddeus Crane and their two children, Lucy and Tad. There are also a plush duck family, the bears, and Mr. Merton Bogart, a troll who lives in a deserted telephone box.

"I say the dolls are not ordinary dolls. I must explain. Mrs. Crane, Melissa Dove Crane, is sixteen inches tall. Permanently aged twenty-two and very beautiful, she belonged to my children's great-great-grandmother and came over from France on the *Great Eastern*. Her wardrobe and accessories would delight any woman. Besides all of this, she has an adorable six-year-old daughter—this is Lucy—and an equally enchanting china baby boy, Tad. Her husband is a dashing officer of the New Hampshire Volunteers.

"On the twenty-fourth of December we set up a miniature room for the dolls' Christmas on top of the Christmas chest which is now empty, of course. I help the dolls decorate their tree. (Melissa says the needles are too prickly for her tiny hands.) The Crane's tree stands twenty inches high and has a string of tiny lights. It looks enchanting in their room which is quite elaborately decorated with doll furniture made to the proper size. There are even little books, real ones, and a glass chandelier made especially for the dolls by some kind friends in the Corning Glass Company. The dolls' own presents are put beneath the tree. The bears and ducklings and Mr. Bogart are brought downstairs—all bringing gifts as well. When all is ready we have our supper. After that we have the dolls' tree, and their presents are opened. There are a number of gifts for the children, too, for the dolls are very generous."

ACCESSORIES TO THE FEAST

Almost as essential to a New England Christmas dinner as the turkey are cranberry sauce and pumpkin pie. Here are Tasha Tudor's family "receipts" for these traditional holiday treats.

CRANBERRY SAUCE

To 2 pounds of cranberries add enough water so that the berries, when pressed down, are not quite covered by it. Add 2 pounds of granulated sugar. Bring to a simmer, skimming occasionally.

Cook over low heat about fifteen minutes until juice jells when dropped on a cold plate. Don't stir too often while cooking.

Pour into a mold and set aside to firm. When ready to serve, place mold in hot water briefly and turn sauce out of mold.

PUMPKIN PIE

Cut a small pumpkin in half, remove seeds, steam pumpkin in covered pot with a little water, and strain the pulp. Take:

1½ cups pulp
⅔ cup light brown sugar
1 teaspoon cinnamon
½ teaspoon ginger
½ teaspoon salt
1½ cups milk
½ cup heavy cream

Mix all these together and bake in an unbaked pie shell at 350° for about thirty-five to forty minutes.

ROASTING THE TURKEY

Most of the traditional New England holiday foods that the Tudors make can easily be made in a modern kitchen, but there will be few readers who can cook their Christmas turkeys as the Tudors do. The turkey is cleaned and stuffed and trussed in the usual manner, and rubbed with bacon fat. It is then placed on the spit of the old-fashioned roasting oven, which is placed in the fireplace of the winter kitchen, where it cooks in a leisurely manner in the heat of the wood fire. Occasionally rotated by hand, and basted, it gradually acquires a rich, golden-brown luster, and fills the house with a tantalizingly delicious aroma.

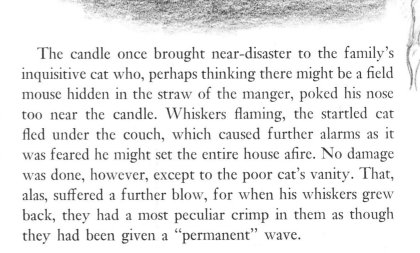

THE CRÈCHE IN THE OVEN

At the side of the great fireplace where the turkey is roasted is a brick-lined bake-oven. In earlier days a wood fire was burned in it until the temperature was raised high enough, and then the embers were removed and the bread was put in it to bake.

Now, with its heavy wooden door removed, the old oven makes a perfect, if unconventional, setting for the Tudors' crèche, or miniature manger scene. Tasha says, "It makes a lovely stable, dark and mysterious. The manger stands in front. A well-loved plush donkey looks at the Baby, along with two woolen lambs from Salisbury, England. A chanticleer stands to one side and in the greens is perched a woolen owl with an especially nice face." The charming, blue-gowned Madonna was made by Tasha Tudor. A single lighted candle sheds a gentle radiance over the scene.

The candle once brought near-disaster to the family's inquisitive cat who, perhaps thinking there might be a field mouse hidden in the straw of the manger, poked his nose too near the candle. Whiskers flaming, the startled cat fled under the couch, which caused further alarms as it was feared he might set the entire house afire. No damage was done, however, except to the poor cat's vanity. That, alas, suffered a further blow, for when his whiskers grew back, they had a most peculiar crimp in them as though they had been given a "permanent" wave.

CHRISTMAS DAY

"And now it is Christmas morning. The stockings are stuffed with most interesting things. These are investigated at once, but the other presents are not opened until later in the day. While I am getting breakfast," says Tasha, "the girls put the turkey on to cook before the open fire in the winter kitchen. We never cook turkey any other way. It just wouldn't taste right, I am sure. The dogs and cats sit about and watch the turkey cooking before the fire, hoping something tasty will be spilled on the hearth. We all help prepare the dinner and sustain the maker of the cranberry sauce when she goes through the trying moment of turning it out.

"Dinner is very special. It is served about two o'clock in the afternoon. The table is spread with the best damask cloth; the green glass finger bowls are brought out and each has a sprig of lemon verbena placed in it. I always think of Christmas when I smell lemon verbena. Dinner is a leisurely and happy affair and the expectation of the tree and presents adds to the joyfulness of the occasion.

"During the morning at odd moments my elder son and I have been trimming the tree. After dinner the other children and aunts and uncles and cousins do the dishes while Seth and I finish the tree-trimming. The ornaments are very old ones—they belonged to the children's great great grandmother—so they must be handled with care. It is one of the few complete collections of such ornaments in existence. Grapes in clusters, roses, apples, oranges, shining balls of all sizes and colors, icicles and tinkling bells, all exquisitely made of heavy glass are carefully hung on the tree. Chains of popcorn and red cranberries, made by the children, are looped from branch to branch, and the 'clear toys,' gingerbread cookies and candy-filled cornucopias complete the picture.

"By the time the evening chores are finished, everyone is in the proper state of excitement. At last the tree is completely decorated and lighted and the presents are piled beneath and around it. Now Seth winds up the antique music box and sets it at *Hark! the Herald Angels Sing*. This is the signal the children have been waiting for. The doors burst open—and there stands the tree in all its shimmering glory. The rest of the evening is spent in that happy enjoyment only Christmas brings."

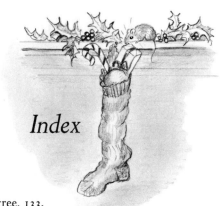

Index

157

ABOUT THE ARTIST

TASHA TUDOR is the very popular author and illustrator of many beautiful books for children. Although born in Boston, she was brought up on a farm in Connecticut and has never lost her love for country life. She paints animals and children with a warmth and delicate charm that have become her trademarks. Tasha Tudor follows in the artistic footsteps of her parents; her mother was Rosamond Tudor, the portrait painter, and her father, W. Starling Burgess, was a famous yacht designer. Tasha Tudor studied art in London and at the Boston Museum School of Fine Arts.

Now, with her own family, she lives in a lovely old red frame farmhouse in New Hampshire. When she is not busy being a housewife and mother and entertaining visiting friends and relatives, Tasha Tudor tends the greenhouse and gardens and looks after the many farm animals—among them ducks, geese, cows, horses, dogs and cats—all "members of the family." Part of each day, she writes and paints at a large and pleasantly cluttered table, permanently set up at one end of her kitchen, where she can enjoy from her window a view of gardens, fields and woods. Yet, somehow, she always finds time for the fun of preparing for festive traditional family celebrations and for enjoying seasonal delights.